Cold Steele

Kimberly Amato

Little Crown Media, LLC

To Bee: for many years of a priceless friendship, staying forever young & of course D&D.

Contents

Foreword

M urder is easy. Cleanup is hard.

No one ever talks about the evacuation of fluids when life ends. There's an inherent indignity that a person goes through when they transition. It's something we are taught to prevent from the time we are potty-trained. We meet death the same way we meet the world: with noise and mess.

Your family or medical staff will need to clean it up. Whether it happens at home or in the hospital, a professional checks vitals and verifies the end. Charts are created and filled out. Information is given to the family about the next steps. Nothing is left to chance. It's a well-thought-out and organized process, removing any and all emotion. It's a one-two punch that every breathing individual on this planet will face. It's inevitable, but our timelines are unknown.

Murder is different. A face in the crowd, seemingly innocuous, makes a choice. Like every other person on this planet, they act according to their desire. They have a story that should clearly explain why they've done the crime. But they're cunning. The words that fall from their lips may run contradictory to the evidence. The laws, human decency . . . all are subject to interpretation in the assailant's mind. In the *Diagnostic and Statistical Manual of Mental Disorders,* or DSM-V, the bible of the American Psychiatric Association, we have a specific classification for them. In society, they're just considered mentally unstable or, at worst psychopathic, with no hope for integration into society. The DSM-V makes that crystal clear.

They are the ones who blend in easily with society with a smile on their face and a helping hand, their eyes scanning each individual as they walk by on the busy New York City streets. Most of the horde have no idea they're being observed. They hustle past with their cell phone pressed tightly to their ear, briefcase slung over their shoulder and a coffee cup in their free hand. But out of the blur, eventually one face slows time.

It could be any number of reasons why they stand out from the other potentials, but most times the hunter couldn't tell you specifically. The pull to their latest victim is as strong as one's desire for water when stranded and floating aimlessly in the Atlantic. They form a list—a catalog if you will—of all those who have come before. The memories come flooding back as they compare the previous ones to the newest. The victim elicits that *je ne sais quoi,* and the hourglass turns over to begin the game again.

The board is set: two players forged in a heated battle of strategy, wits, and survival. The victim goes about her day, unaware that someone is logging her trips to the gym, to that favorite grocery store, to the theater. Her home becomes their favorite place. Their pleasure is elicited by watching her sleep, and they crawl into her bed when she's not around and leave their mark without her knowing. Each step, each link in the chain of information, gets them one step closer to the climactic confrontation.

Sometimes a rapport will be built, the killer wanting to be even closer if the situation provides access. At their heart, the psychopath is a manipulative, Oscar-winning actor. They can portray anything convincingly with the life of their victim as their trophy. Calmly, they wait for the right moment with the least interference from the outside world for the final play.

It's then that the more difficult elements come to the forefront. There can be no hesitation once the decision has been made. There can be no turning around or stopping midway. Their tools must be brought with them, or the room must be set precisely to exact specifications. They must be aware of the prying eyes of those nearby and how sound might travel to them. A methodical process to finish the job is paramount. If interrupted, a messy and quick death would be required. Tying up loose ends would be difficult, and the true essence of the mission will have failed. The hunt then starts up again immediately to replace their displeasure from the previous choice.

But they are rarely interrupted. There's no uncertainty as they watch you from the park bench. No doubt when they laugh with you over a dinner date. There's no fear of being caught as their lips crush each other's in the elevator on the way to her floor. There's no concern as she pulls them drunkenly to her room.

She sloppily swats at clothing, trying to remove the barrier. The killer tosses a duffel bag to the floor before fumbling with their belt. There's no hesitation when lifting her up and slamming her to the bed. The tearing of clothing, however expensive, is inconsequential to their needs. The feeling of skin pressed up against skin elicits pleasure, but it's not enough for them. It's never enough.

She begs, her slurred words demanding pleasure. There's no room for uncertainty as she grabs the killer's back and tries to control the situation. Knowing full well the time is close, they take her. With every thrust, her voice becomes more ragged and sweat forms on her brow. That doesn't concern the assailant. They feel themselves growing rigid, their hands fisting the pillows and sheets below.

Before they can lose their edge, their hands wrap around her throat and squeeze as pleasure radiates throughout their entire body. The woman's eyes widen with fear as her fists punch the arms above her. Her strength, her resistance, was all planned for. That's why they went for drinks: to take the edge off. Her defensive blows slow as her breathing stops. They finish and remove themselves.

Cleanup begins in earnest now. Time is not a concern or worry. The most beautiful works of art take time, and this one will be a masterpiece. Opening the bag, they pull out their small bottles to clean. A funnel, a small bottle of a mixed solution, a rag, and a small switchblade are all the tools they need. They fill the victim again with the liquid, wiping her skin with a wet rag to cleanse her of their touch. Once that's complete, they carve a small heart in-between her breasts before pouring the rest of the solution down the shower drain.

After dressing themselves and packing up their tools, they pull out their calling card. The murderer places one white carnation on her stomach with the petals touching the bottom point of the heart. They've given her the ultimate gift, and she accepted. Pulling out their cell phone, they take a few pictures before walking out of the room as if nothing happened, duffel bag over their shoulder as they saunter to the elevator, passing other patrons on the way. No one is the wiser that a dead woman is still somewhat warm behind one of the doors.

Walking back into the streets of the city that never sleeps, the faces once again blur as their desire has been satiated. The varying societal levels are meaningless to this predator. Job titles, money, or notoriety can't save you when yours is the face that comes into focus. It's all about methodology, precision, and power. Everyone is below them in the playing field of life. In the killer's mind, being chosen and defiled is the most precious gift they can give the victim. The sounds, mess, and possible fighting during the act is the victim's gift back to the assailant. Every part becomes the musicians in the orchestra playing the most exotic, euphoric, and erotic arrangement. It quenches the thirst until the urge rears its ugly head again.

Most people move around the world like cattle on their way to slaughter. Death has no problem taking anyone at any time, but most people meet it at the end of a long journey. For those unlucky enough to be the face in focus, their life has already met its end. They just haven't played their final song . . . yet.

Chapter One

Standing in front of the darkened room, I'm slowly pacing back and forth between two large, white projection screens. The one on my left shows a ghastly murder scene: a Black woman on her back with a sheet covering her legs, a white carnation over her stomach and a heart cut into her skin between her blurred-out breasts. Her glazed-over eyes stare at nothing, her neck covered in blackish bruises in the shape of a hand.

"Reyna Lewis was staying in the Bogart Hotel downtown. She was a professor from Maryland State University visiting the city with her friend, Eve Quid, and Eve's sister Jillian." The words fall out of my mouth quickly, nerves from engaging in public speaking etching their way into my tone. "She was murdered the day before she was to return home to Maryland. Eve found her body the next morning when Reyna didn't answer her phone."

My eyes glance over the packed auditorium of John Jay College of Criminal Justice, room L63. More than two hundred people cram into the space, listening to me spout off about a three-year-old cold case. In some ways, it's exhilarating to be back in my alma mater, but it's also terrifying because of the accusatory glances of those judging me for just trying to do the right thing. I click another button on the remote and the screen on my right comes to life with a typed-out list.

"We know she met someone at a bar the first night she was in the city. Based on Jillian Quid's statement, we know that she ran into this individual three additional times. The final time, Jillian told police they were at a bar drinking to their last night in town. Ms. Quid was inebriated and unable to narrow down the time frame in which Reyna returned to her room. We do know the killer left his calling card on her skin between the flower and the heart." I walk over to the screen and stand below it.

"The list you see here is all we have to go on. White male, could be middle-aged, average height and build. No one could remember him walking in or out of the hotel. There were no cameras in the hallway and no witnesses were sober enough to pick him out on the bar's surveillance. Even the bartenders that evening state everyone was the same—a customer needing a drink. He was your everyday individual who worked a job and went home. The only concrete information we know for sure is his affinity for white carnations and carving up the victim's skin." Walking back to the podium, I wave at a professor by the light switch. He flips two up, and the entire room illuminates.

"I could go on about the evidence, or lack thereof, in this case, but I want to hear from you. What do you see? What do you want to know? Ask me whatever comes to your mind." I look around the room. Silence. I see a few people lingering over the crime scene image. "I can switch to another image if you would like. Anyone?"

Again, I'm met with silence. Finally, I see a hand gingerly raise in the back of the room.

"In the back. Could you please stand up so I can see you?"

A young man, very tall, wearing jeans and a polo shirt that barely covers his torso, stands up. "I look at the scene and I want to know if she recently had intercourse or was assaulted," he says as he shifts nervously from one foot to the other.

"Good start." I move to the front of the podium to make it more intimate. My nerves are long forgotten. I focus on the student who remains standing, waiting for my answer. "According to the coroner's report, there was evidence of sexual intercourse before her death. Due to the lack of vaginal tearing, one could assume it leans more to the consensual side, but we can't be certain either way."

"Fluids?" the young man squeaks.

"Inconclusive." I reach over the podium and grab the remote. I aim it at the screen to my right and bring up another image of the body on the coroner's table. "The killer fully cleaned his victim. If there was any DNA on the body, his efforts contaminated and degraded it."

The young man sits down as he digests the information. Another hand pops up closer to the front. An older woman stands, her glasses reflecting the lights above, preventing me from seeing her face clearly.

"In the image you have on the screen, the bed looks a mess, but the room looks clean. I would look at the rest of the room to see if the killer cleaned up or left fingerprints or some other evidence behind," she says.

"Crime scene was normal. Nothing out of the ordinary. Her larger suitcase was packed. Her smaller carryon was open on a luggage rack. We assume she was planning on packing the rest of her toiletries and clothing in the morning before leaving. Nothing to indicate the perpetrator cleaned anything up but the victim herself."

"Fingerprints . . ." she continues.

"We dusted the entire room. Found several of them. It's a hotel room with a myriad of people coming and going on a daily basis. We also spoke to housekeeping. Due to Reyna being a rather neat guest, they barely cleaned her room. They just made the bed and put out more soap and other products. Being that several people entered and exited the room daily, any fingerprints found could easily be fought over in court. For it to be worthwhile to the case, it needs to be found in direct proximity or on the body."

The door creaks open, and I see Frankie Ryan standing at the top of the stairs. She slowly descends toward me. "In regard to fingerprints, you should remember they are not a one-stop shop for a conviction. This isn't a Hollywood script; it's reality. Even if you get a usable print, it's not the beginning and end-all of a case. The computers are not going to spit out an answer the minute you drop it in there. You might get a hit, but you can't use it as your definitive proof. You need to build a case around everything. Make sure you uncover as much as humanly possible before handing it over to the district attorney or your bosses. A fingerprint's just the beginning. You need to answer the how, but sometimes the why is the most difficult to ascertain. Which is why I will now hand you over to my esteemed colleague, Dr. Francesca Ryan."

The audience claps as Frankie walks in front of the podium and looks at the two images. She picks up the remote and turns both screens off. I lean against the wall by the descending staircase, close enough to be part of the conversation, but far enough away to give her some space.

"Detective Steele told you about the Carnation Killer's scene, but for me the bigger picture is the psychology behind his actions. Four victims, all different heights, religions, and ethnicities. Some were from out of town, some lived here in the city, and some out in the suburbs. None of them interacted or crossed paths. Their ages ranged from twenties to late fifties. It's as if he doesn't have a pattern at all."

"But he has to. Even randomness is a pattern," a male student says from the front row.

"In theory, yes." Frankie walks right up to the student and stares at him. He squirms under her attention. "But what is that pattern? Is it physical? Psychological? Does he stalk them? How long does he give them to live? What tools does he use consistently? Why? Can you answer anything other than a random pattern is in theory, a pattern?"

"No, ma'am."

"That's the point. We don't know. At this current time, the evidence doesn't back up any one specific theory. The mind of a psychopath or sociopath is similar to a huge puzzle. Now, if you bought one at a store, we could put the framing together and then fill in the picture according to the layout on the box. These individuals seem to be normal. They work among us, live next door, and give no indication that they are outside the parameters of the puzzle. Yet, upon further inspection, we see they have no borders. They have no set image that they live by. They just seem to exist in their own world with the rest of us as simple spectators."

A hand pops up in the center of the room. Frankie acknowledges him with a nod, and the gentleman stands up. His short haircut, jeans, shirt, and suit jacket scream professional but casual.

"As a psychologist, how do you study these types of criminals? How do you create a profile for them?"

"That depends. If I get to sit in a room with the accused, I could follow Hare's Psychology Checklist. I'd be able to see the shallow emotions, the traits that are more prominent in a case like this. In most scenarios, however, I'm given images like the ones you saw on the screens earlier. I'll have access to all evidence that has been collected, and somehow, I have to put all of that into an assessment or profile. How do I do it? Very meticulously. You study every photograph closely. You scour through your books to see if anything clicks. It's a long, arduous process, but it's what you have to do."

Frankie turns her attention from the individual who asked the question back to the whole room.

"Psychology is not an exact science. I can sit here and tell you all the tricks I've learned over the years in the field, but it wouldn't help you. They're *my* tricks that I developed through *my* own personal experiences. We must be as accurate as we can be, and most of the time that means leaving a lot to interpretation. Gray areas exist because life isn't always black-and-white. For those of you going into some kind of police work, you will have books full of rules and regulations to follow. The rest of us *have* to read between the lines. We can't just say 'he shot someone' and move on. We *have* to know why. We *have* to figure out what his mindset might have been during the act itself. That information could change the course of the trial itself, but more importantly, it could determine sentencing. The motive—the reasons behind every act—means a mentally ill individual could get the medical help they need versus punitive punishment and possible recidivism."

A faculty member walks across the stage and stands next to Frankie. He's talking to the crowd, but my focus is on my fiancé. She hates speaking in front of others more so than I do, but she handled her five minutes rather well. I just have to get through the after-presentation refreshments in the adjacent room and everything will be back to normal. Frankie walks over and stands next to me as the speaker wraps up the presentation and dismisses the group.

"You used most of the time we were allotted," she whispers, a half smirk etched on her face.

"Blame the nerves," I say with smile. If we weren't in our professional roles, I would kiss her for emphasis.

"Well, you do tend to babble when they kick in," Frankie says and nudges me with her shoulder.

"Excuse me, Dr. Ryan?" A student stands patiently waiting to talk to her.

"Yes?" She turns in the student's direction.

"Your fiancé is a very smart woman," a man says behind me.

Frankie's conversation fades away as I turn around. The gentleman stands taller than my five-foot-nine frame. His dark blue jeans, button-down shirt, and a black sport coat are pure hipster. His black Timberland boots seemed almost out of place. His bald head reflects the LED lights from the ceiling, and sunglasses block the color of his eyes.

"Yes, she is," I say, trying to decipher the meaning behind his words.

"I'm being rude; forgive me. I've read all about this case. It's fascinating really," he says, holding his hand out for me to shake. I accept it.

"True crime junkie or professional?" I say, feeling his firm grip around my hand. My tone lighter and more relaxed than before.

"A bit of both, I'm afraid. I teach various psychology classes to the undergraduates and a few graduates. Got an email and here I am."

"Graduates? What class?"

"This semester, Clinical Interviewing."

"Oh, God, I hated that class. My friend and I would start a conversation that would last the entire lesson just to stop our professor from talking."

"It is a rather droll class." He laughs as his eyes never leave mine. "I'm surprised you didn't get kicked out or end up in the dean's office."

"Nah, we weren't horrible. Just annoying. Rite of passage, you know?"

"I can certainly understand that," he says in a hushed tone that makes me a bit uncomfortable.

"Well, thank you for teaching the future generations of New Yorkers. Did you enjoy the talk?" I change the subject as my eyes dart to Frankie, who's standing off to the side in a conversation of her own. Her hands animatedly wave about.

"Yes, ma'am. I was surprised the press didn't leak more information regarding the crime scenes when they happened. I'm even more surprised you shared the case with us here," he says.

"Well, at the time there was so much misinformation out there we were concerned about reality being lost in all the speculation—"

"So, the department held it back," he interjects.

"Not so much held back as it was conscious sharing. Like the images I showed of the crime scene, those are part of the public file. We released things on our website, various government pages. All readily accessible for the media and community," I answer.

"Based on that statement, one can assume there is more hidden behind the scenes."

"I wish I could tell you, but it's still an active investigation."

"You think he'll ever be caught?"

"I think so. As technology advances, it helps us close older cases with new methods. One always has to have a positive outlook on things like this," I answer truthfully. In the last year or so, I've seen amazing things from hard-working people in the department—everyone from Lillian Brown in forensics to Logan Pevy in tech. There's always a new angle on a crime scene. It might not always work right away, like with the Carnation Killer case, but it works in time.

"I don't know. I think this one might just get away with it. He seems calculated, smarter than the average criminal. Maybe a bit of Jack the Ripper mixed with the Zodiac Killer," he tosses out.

"Those are rather big shoes to fill for a man who plays with flowers. You're right, though; he is smart. We're more patient. We can wait," I answer a little firmly than before.

"But at what cost? How many more people need to die? I don't mean to sound disheartening or crass, but you've got four bodies on your table. How many more do you need before this case gets taken away from you and your team? Your job is to find killers, not waste time while you attempt to figure out puzzles. This individual seems better at committing the crimes than you are at solving them. The evidence never lies."

"He won't stop until we catch him. It's basic psychology."

"The original detective, Gino Reyes—your old partner I believe—said the same thing. Drank himself to death after he retired. Maybe it's time to admit that you need help and let someone else take over? It's not your fault, but poster child for the NYPD or not, you aren't any closer to catching him than you were when he took a hiatus."

"He did take a break, and I know the trail might appear colder than usual, but I don't give up. Especially when a narcissistic limp dick needs to get off on hurting women. I became a detective to stop people like him, not walk away from a difficult scenario."

"Sounds like you should put that out to the media: 'Detective Steele Challenges Carnation Killer. News at eleven,'" he says, laughing to himself.

"Look, I appreciate you attending the conference, but don't try—"

"The reception is in the next room, Jasmine. Shall we go?" Frankie says, her hand gingerly touching my elbow. My eyes firmly bore holes into the male asshole in front of me.

"It was a pleasure talking with you, detective," he says before he casually walks away. Frankie tugs at my elbow and I turn to face her. "Are you alright?"

"Sure, just another day and another dipshit telling me how to do my job. Even if he is a bit right," I say, resigned.

"What do you mean?" she asks, lifting my chin so my eyes meet hers.

"Maybe it's time to send this over to the FBI."

"Maybe you could talk to Karina and ask her," Frankie suggests.

"Well, Agent Marlow is on a much-deserved vacation after helping us with Garrison. Besides, she has her own serial killer to catch in Seattle. Maybe we just need fresh eyes," I say, looking around at the now empty lecture room.

"Then let's go deal with the other presenters over refreshments before heading back to work."

"Or maybe you can . . ."

"Jasmine, please don't leave me here with other psychology professionals," she begs. "Everyone is analyzing everything we say or do. It's rather unpleasant."

"You're guilty of it too!" I retort.

She laughs in reply. "I was trained that way! Look, it's easier to handle the scrutiny with someone by my side. Please?"

My cell phone rings before I can answer. Captain Zeile's name flashes on the screen, and I look up apologetically at Frankie. Looks like drinks with the psychological crew will have to wait.

"Steele," I answer, still holding her hand.

"Are you free?" he asks.

"Presentation is over and I didn't paint anyone's shoes with my stomach contents. I'd say it was a resounding success," I answer happily.

"Good, get back to the station. One PP is getting on my ass about your paperwork from the Garrison case. There's also another matter we need to discuss," he finishes.

"On my way," I say and hang up.

"Let me walk you out." Frankie links her arm in mine. "You know it's rude to just hang up the phone without saying goodbye."

"But they do it in all the cool movies," I answer as we walk up the stairs.

"This is real life, darling. We show courtesy and compassion. We don't have a magic phone booth or some gun that puts demons back into the ground . . . although that last one is a sword now."

"Aww, you've been binge-watching *Doctor Who* and *Wynonna Earp*! I'm so proud." I laugh as we reach the hallway.

"Yes, well, someone has to understand what the hell you all are talking about at the dinner table. You, Chase, and Hadley drive me crazy. Besides, she's dragging us to Comic-Con this year so I might as well educate myself. You better make sure you get those dates in October off," she says before kissing my chapped lips. "Now go before I drag you in there with me."

I lean forward and rub my lips on hers for Chapstick. She pushes me off with a grimace and smacks my left shoulder. "You goof! Go serve and protect . . . yourself from papercuts." She laughs as she walks into the adjacent room.

As I reach the escalator, my phone beeps. A text message from my recuperating partner Will Everts floats along the screen. Opening it, I see an image of Will standing with his hands on his hips in a *Superman* pose outside of the hospital, the words *Finally Free* underneath it. It was touch-and-go for a while, but he pulled through and apparently is headed home. I'm sure his wife Mia and their daughters will drive him crazy for a long time.

***

The media still hangs around the precinct like parasitic bacteria trying to gather more information about the Garrison case. Garrison is the man whose son drove drunk and killed my brother and his wife. The man who tried to ruin me and take my life. The man on a ladder of corruption that ranged from low-level gang members to Judge Killian. The press made us darlings, but none of us wanted to be.

It's been a hot minute, but as the US District Attorney, the FBI, and even the CIA keep digging, more names are called with indictments. I knew Irving Garrison had some reach, but it turns out he was only part of a much larger machine. He remained loyal, but the low-level associates sang like canaries. The more names they gave up, the higher up the chain it went. This past week, three congressmen were connected and arrested. They proclaim their innocence, but according to Logan, the evidence is too damning.

The worst part is that it seems never-ending. My piece of the case is over. I've testified. I'm trying to get back to the everyday. I'm even in therapy to deal with the anger that remains, which helps with the insecurity that pops up every now and again. I just want to get back to helping people. But with greater scrutiny comes more intense paperwork. Dotting my i's and crossing my t's was not why I got a badge. Indirectly, murder in my area is down. So, I'll take it.

Walking through the pen to my office, it's hard not to notice the new energy that radiates in the place. Blame the new captain for all this hard-nosed, no bullshit, wall-of-blue attitude. He's already forced a few transfers of those members not making the cut. Everyone knows of the one probie he made cry in the middle of the squad room. The story has changed the more it it's been told, but the kid was removed from his duties as an officer. That's where the story ends. No idea if there was an appeal, but the new boss is cleaning house. After Captain Udall was murdered and a few of our own were arrested for corruption, he's doing his best to clean our precinct's name. Even if that means pimping out his not-so-favorite anti-social detective—namely, me.

"Detective?" Zeile's voice echoes from across the hall. "Come here for a minute."

The captain's office has changed in the past few months. The photos of Tyler Udall with his friends, various other officers, and his wife are long gone. Now, New York Yankees paraphernalia seems to cover almost every wall in all its nauseating glory, the worst being a 2000 World Series Champions banner hanging up near the coat rack. Any other indications of who the man is are hidden from view. No personal photos or speaking of his family. I don't even know if he's in a serious relationship or married.

"Sir," I say, trying to avoid looking at Derek Jeter's smiling face on the wall behind his desk.

"We've been getting some calls requesting interviews with you," he begins. "I've informed the higher-ups that it isn't in our best interest for you to sit down and discuss things."

"Thank you." The stress in my shoulders relaxes a bit.

"I learned my lesson last time." He shakes his head.

"They shouldn't have asked about Frankie."

"She was part of the investigation."

"Yes, she was. If the reporter was asking about the case, I'd answer. Prodding me for questions of who's on top, are you the male in the relationship, whatever . . . it was a bit out of line."

"I would have handled it."

"I did."

"Using Mr. Pevy to expose that the reporter was homophobic was illegal, and you used department hours. You could have been disciplined." He walks around his desk, his glasses sliding to rest on the tip of his nose as he glares at me.

"Not at all. Logan worked from home, used previous clips that had aired in the past, and brought up old Tweets and Facebook posts, nothing that wasn't already in the public domain." I shrug.

"Just because you can doesn't mean you should. Next time you cut the interview short and come to me. I'll handle it. Are we clear?"

"Yes, sir," I say, somewhat happy that this conversation is over. Morally, I regretted exposing the reporter for the hypocrite he was . . . but it didn't make it right. You have to rise above the vitriol in order to better the world around you. Easily said via platitudes but difficult to execute in real time.

"In the meantime, Detective Everts is still out. I've got a new detective filling in until he clears medical and all the other happy horseshit. I'm assigning her to you for the time being. She has an active case the higher-ups want closed as soon as possible. Maybe she'll help you deal with all that damn paperwork you have to finish." He waves his hand in the air as he sits down at his desk, effectively dismissing me.

"Cap, just remember that I'm meeting Frankie at a venue for the wedding tomorrow. Might not be able to answer my phone, so text if it's an emergency, okay?" I say, slowly backing away.

"Yes, yes, now go," he says while reading something on his desk.

✴✴✴

Walking into my office, I see a young Black woman sitting in Will's chair. Her eyes peer through her frameless glasses as she frantically writes some notes. The free-flowing curls of her jet-black hair bounce around as she works. Her entire body is engrossed in the task at hand. The sound of the door closing behind me pulls her gaze up to meet mine.

"Detective Steele?" she asks with a slight uptick in her voice.

"That's me. You're the new temp?" I say. I want her to know that I already have a partner.

"Temp?" she says with slight confusion in her voice.

"You're sitting at my partner's desk."

"Captain Zeile said I should sit here until Detective Everts comes back," she says, finally understanding my comments.

"Excellent." The sarcasm oozes in my tone more than it should. "You have a name?"

"Sydney Locke."

"Jasmine Steele." She smiles in acknowledgment before turning her attention back to her notes.

"What're you working on?" I say. I toss my jacket on my chair before sitting on the edge of my desk.

"A case that isn't sitting well with me," she answers, never looking up from the page.

"This wouldn't be the case the man on high wants finished quickly, would it?" I answer with air quotes and hand motions.

Sydney leans back in the chair, her attention fully on me now. She closes the file but never breaks eye contact. It's obvious she is not about to trust me regardless of my name in this place or in the media.

"Answer me one question, and then, maybe, I'll answer yours." She intertwines her fingers over her waist.

"Shoot."

"Why did you go to the film set when you knew shit was going to hit the fan? Did you not graduate the same academy I did?"

"I did, and I was fourth in my class."

"I graduated first in mine."

"And this 'my-standing-is-better-than-your-standing' is important why?"

"Well, that stunt you pulled put women back at least three decades," she says, shrugging her shoulders. "Maybe times have changed since your day, but I don't remember the suicide mission class."

"One of my best friends was in danger . . ."

"You should have pulled yourself off the case or told Detective Everts. Seriously, what is it with women thinking they should run before thinking? We're smarter than that." She smirks at me.

It's then I truly take her in: The heeled boots giving her about three more inches in height. The classy outfit with a modern fashionable flair to it. Simple accessories and minimal makeup. Her light brown eyes highlight some freckles on her nose, and just barely hidden under the collar of her button-down shirt is a tattoo. This woman exudes confidence as well as a small rebelliousness. I like her already.

"I wasn't in a good headspace. Made a rash decision to deal with the situation. Right or wrong, it's over, and I have a partner I can trust to always have my back."

She stands and, with three of her shorter strides, ends up in front of me. She extends her hand into the space between us.

"You're forgiven."

"I'm forgiv— "

She cuts me off. "We all make stupid mistakes. Just nice to hear someone admit it."

"Admitting mistakes gets you sued." I offer my hand and she shakes it firmly. Her chipped nails dig a bit into my skin, forcing me to let go earlier than I intended.

"If you screwed up enough to be sued, you wouldn't be working here," she comments before resting against Will's desk. She leans back, never taking her eyes off me as she grabs the file on her desk. "The DA wants to fast-track this case, but something's not right. I had hoped to talk with Detective Everts, but that's not going to happen for obvious reasons."

She holds the file out for me. Instead of taking it, I walk over to the whiteboard filled with Irving Garrison connections. The old information has been on here for so long I don't even remember what any other case looks like. So many years of my life all focused on one inanimate dry erase board.

But it's time to move on. Grabbing the eraser, I make quick work of cleaning it off. Within seconds, the entire surface is clear. The dual meaning isn't lost on me, but it takes a few seconds and a deep breath to put the eraser back.

"Write it out," I say to Sydney, handing her a black marker.

She drops the file back on Will's desk, walks to the board, and starts writing down all the aspects of the crime in the left column.

"If you need the file at any time, I'll grab it for you."

"Trust me, I know it by heart at this point." She writes the name Douglas Keets on the board in all capital letters. I grab the file and flip through it.

"According to this, Keets had no priors or even a juvenile record. How did you manage to get your hands on that information?"

"He gave us permission to dig into everything. Signed a waiver with his lawyer present."

"Everyone has skeletons in their closet. Risky signing a document like that."

"He maintains his innocence and probably assumed the information we found would exonerate him."

"I assume it hasn't," I answer, my head still in the file.

"Very astute, detective," Sydney says sarcastically. "The psychiatrist on his case said he believes Keets suffered from first-break schizophrenia. Legally, he should be placed in a facility for a competency exam."

"You wouldn't still be on this case if it was that simple. Cynical me says they'd medicate him in Riker's so he seems more normal. Cheaper, easier, and gets a conviction on the charge the DA actually feels he can prosecute and win. The question is why? How is it being fast-tracked and by whom?" I close the file and place it on my desk.

"That depends on a few things. Keets was honorably discharged from the Marine Corps last year. He had some difficulty getting back on his feet, so he moved in with his mother and stepfather."

She writes their names under victims.

"He's accused of killing his family? That changes the ballgame."

"That's why he told us to dig. So, I did. Keets was starting to get back on his feet working with wounded vets at a church. It didn't pay much, but according to the priest, Keets was getting as much help as he was giving."

"We both know personal opinions are biased and unreliable. What does the evidence tell you?" I ask.

"I never said he didn't do it. I just don't think he can be held accountable for his actions." She crosses the office and pulls out another stack of files. Dropping them on Will's desk, she spreads them out over the desktop, opening several to tagged pages. Various images, medical files and military history are mixed up with several blacked-out sections.

"According to his medical records, there was no indication of mental disease or a history of it in his family." She hands me a piece of paper with his vital statistics and chunks of information redacted from view.

"He was thirty-seven. Normally first breaks happen before the age of thirty," I say to myself.

"Yes, but men usually exhibit symptoms earlier in their lives than women. So, theoretically, this individual should have shown some kind of psychosis by the time he entered the Marines."

"Not necessarily. It could have appeared after he was deployed," I say.

"True, but given the stress required to perform at the high level that his position demanded, the break should have happened sooner."

My gut says she's right, but each human being has a different response to stress. It's why psychology is such a gray area; it has to be considered on a case-by-case basis. This guy should have broken sooner rather than later. I don't think he would have survived one day in Iraq, let alone the full extent of his tour if he was mentally ill. My God, he would have endangered his entire platoon every moment he was there.

Dropping the piece of paper on the desk, I scan several others. My eyes fall on his military photo and some notes scribbled on the photocopied page. He never finished his second tour but was honorably discharged.

"Any symptoms or triggers listed in his file?"

"None that I can tell. His files were heavily redacted, as you can see." She picks up another photocopied piece of paper. It's a photo. She hands it to me, and all I can focus on is a bloody and battered Keets in his uniform. "He was injured in the line of duty. Ambushed while doing a routine sweep. Ended up losing his leg to infection from shrapnel. The mission, who was there, what exactly happened—it's all hidden under black lines."

"Let me guess: you want to know what happened but the Department of Justice and the Pentagon have been less than helpful."

"They keep transferring me to the other without any care in the world. It's as if once a soldier is home, they're no longer the government's problem."

"That's exactly how it is," I say, putting the image down. "Okay. Evidence is king. If it points to Keets, then he's going to pay for the crime."

Sydney reaches into her bag again and pulls out another file. She holds it to her chest for a few seconds before handing it over to me. "What if someone pushed him to it? Or at least primed the situation, knowing the outcome."

Flipping it open, I see a grainy security footage screen capture of an older man similar in height who resembles Keets. The name next to the image is Otto Keets, implicated in several robberies, extortion, sexual assault, and a litany of other charges. Looking through the family history, I see that Douglas Keets is a distant cousin.

"Before you ask, he might not be a direct blood cousin, but Otto was a fixture in Douglas's life. He kept tabs on his deployment; they had consistent contact via emails or social media. Having talked with neighbors, Otto was seen. Regularly," she adds.

"Doesn't prove much though," I answer.

"Maybe not, but it shows a pattern of being connected to some rather unsavory characters." Sydney spits this out, and I find myself smiling at her words. "Did I say something?"

"My mother used to say the kids I hung out with were unsavory characters. Even after all of them became successful, she still didn't like them." I look up at the confused detective. I clear my throat and look back to the file. "No history of employment? Didn't the detectives wonder how he could afford a two-bedroom apartment in Chelsea?"

"Sure, just not the ones on this case."

She takes the file from my hand and drops it back on her desk. Sydney walks to the board and writes some more information down quickly. "According to my informant, Otto was moving tainted money using Douglas's mom's job as a bank teller. When Douglas came home, he stumbled upon what his mother was doing. He convinced her to come clean to the cops."

"So, kid comes home, with possible trauma buried under those redacted lines, has the wherewithal to talk his mother out of a money laundering bid? I don't know. That sounds too far of a stretch."

"He was struggling though. There's an elderly neighbor across the hall. She said Douglas would help her with her bags all the time. She noticed him being quiet but respectful. One day she made him tea and told him to sit down. The two of them talked about his deployment. The minute she pushed him about life now that he was home, Douglas excused himself."

"If everything you're telling me is accurate, he doesn't sound like someone suffering from schizophrenia. Any psychological testing done?"

"No, not at all. Douglas refused all tests, needles . . . anything that he deemed too personal. All I know is his mother left a message with the detective listed on the casefile about coming in to discuss Otto Keets. The next day, the whole family is wiped out and we have a retired Marine who has no memory of the incident at hand."

"Where's Otto Keets now?"

"Allegedly on business overseas. He was here for the funerals but informed the district attorney it would be too painful to watch the trial. Since the evidence was damning enough, the prosecution let him go. I have a suspicion he's behind this. I know the evidence says it's Douglas, but we both know things aren't always as they appear."

"One of these things is not like the other . . . one of these things is not the same," I sing softly to myself as I scan the board. Sydney stares at me, her face once again riddled with confusion. "Not a *Sesame Street* fan?" I ask, and she shakes her head. I continue. "Think about the case as a whole. DNA doesn't lie. It's hard as hell to fake unless you have some genius intelligence and a massive lab somewhere. Either way you go, the DA has a perp he can get a conviction against. The other is circumstantial. No testing. Detachment, aggressiveness . . ."

"I did some research and Douglas wasn't on any medication, but . . ."

"Post-traumatic stress disorder," I blurt out, cutting her off. "A vet suffers in silence. There are support groups all over. If you can find someone willing to talk to you about his case, then you can possibly piece together what might have happened. It wouldn't be too difficult for Otto to set off the right triggers and put his cousin in a full-fledged response."

"But it explains a lot more, including the memory loss."

"It's almost impossible to prove without a competency exam or at least a proper psychological assessment," I add.

"Maybe Dr. Ryan could take a look at these files?" she asks me. Instantly, I wonder if she was just sharing this case with me due to my connection. Frankie is one of the best there is, and we don't hide our relationship. We're professional, and in the past she's gone on the stand to defend someone I gathered evidence against. It rarely comes between us, but neither one of us has ever condoned using our connection to garner special assistance.

"I can't ask her that. If it was an assigned case that's one thing, but I can't—"

"I'll talk to her. All I'm asking is for an introduction," Sydney continues.

"Call the office. Anyone in that office will investigate it if there's just cause," I say. Sydney continues to stare at the board, arms crossed and defiant. She's angry at my answer, and I understand her response. "How many years have you been a detective?" I ask.

"That doesn't change my ability to do the job!"

"I didn't say it did." I lower my voice, trying to bring a calmness to the conversation. "We have to work together, and it's my job to make sure your concerns are brought to the right people. If I bring this to Doctor Ryan, the defense could use it against you. Lord knows they've tried against me and my team. We've got years of experience getting around the bullshit. You don't."

"Silence is key," she answers quickly.

"The walls have ears. Trust me, nothing stays quiet for too long. It's too obvious a connection. I know you're stressed and this case needs to be handled as soon as possible, but you have to do it right. From someone who ran into the devil's den without backup and almost paid the price . . ."

"I get it. Doesn't mean I like it." Sydney erases the board quickly, drops the eraser into the tray below, and cleans the files off Will's desk. Her frustration oozes off her body in waves. She's a smart detective, but you can tell she's green.

My old captain would have loved training her. Tyler Udall's first lesson to me was to always clean up after myself. *"You never know who's watching you, Jasmine."* The second was never stop learning or innovating. You're dead in the water otherwise. I can see that in her. Her ability to hide her emotions will come in time. It takes experience, and sometimes a case that hits you hard. Or maybe two . . . or three.

Sitting at my desk looking over the folders piled high on my left, I remember learning that lesson when I was in graduate school. Nothing like trying to keep a straight face as an inmate pleases himself in front of you. Each time I would go on the prison ward and ask if he had completed his task in crayon, he would ignore me. The first time I was in complete shock. I had no idea how to handle it. I stumbled over my words, and he had the response he wanted. I remember taking such a hot shower that night my skin was dark red. I needed to remove the feeling of that man ogling me, objectifying everything that I was. It was an impossible task.

This continued for almost a week. I found myself asking him inane questions from whatever psychological exam I was administering. He'd refuse to answer simple questions intended to gauge his intelligence, and his family history was incomplete; I had nothing to report to my bosses. I never got any answers, but he always requested my presence on the ward. If there was any question on any form, he would request my presence. Like a trained seal, I complied.

During the second week, something in me broke. Meetings with the inmate were cut short if I went to see him at all. I always locked eyes with him but remained calm and unfeeling. After his last refusal to fill out a simple form, I went to my supervisor with what I had. I had wide-eyed hopes of helping people, but in this case, he didn't want it. So, somewhere in this man's file, for all the world to read publicly, is a psychological report on his desire for pleasure over medical assistance. I'm sure it was read at his trial. Either way, that one-page report is a part of his medical record forever.

I didn't want to write it. I didn't even want to be a part of the situation, but we all have to play the cards we're dealt. I learned the hard way that not everyone will respect you and not everyone wants your help.

"Integrity." The word rolls out of my mouth as the memories of my internship stay fresh in my mind.

"Excuse me?" Sydney's voice bounces around the room.

"It's what separates us from them. No matter how much a criminal pushes, we stay the course, no matter how difficult it is." I look up from my desk and see Sydney staring at me, her emotions still etched on her face. I write something down on my Post-it notepad before tossing the pad to Sydney. "Call Agent Karina Marlow. We worked together in the past; she has more resources that could help you. If she doesn't answer, then call Dr. Ryan's office."

"What happened to muddying up the waters?"

"She's a Fed. I'm only recommending her because of the military connection. She might be able to get more solid information for you. Besides, I'm not engaged to her. Less mud, more of a morning fog before it burns off."

"And if I call Dr. Ryan?"

"We'll deal with that bridge if we have to cross it."

"Thanks," she says, tearing off the number before tossing the pad back to me.

I catch the pad and dump it back on the mess that is my desk. There's so much against the two of us at the moment from the outside world. If I can help her, I will. She seems like a smart one, but time will tell if she can handle the bullshit that is a patriarchal society. It's harder in here than it ever will be on the streets.

Chapter Two

A banging on the front door pulls me out of peaceful slumber, alone. Frankie's probably getting Chase ready for school. More banging on the poor, red, fiberglass door. I jump up and run down the stairs two at a time in my pajamas.

"Jazz, are you in there?" This time the doorbell rings. "Dammit, Jazz, I need your help. Like now!" The doorbell chimes again.

"Hold on!" I scream as I unlock the bolt before swinging the door open. Hadley stands there in a baseball cap, sunglasses, and a black leather jacket. She looks the worse for wear as she pushes by me and into the house.

"You have any coffee?" She paces into the kitchen.

"You know where the pods are," I say, locking the door. Leaning against it, I watch Hadley rush around the kitchen.

Hadley's career is on the upward swing lately, and with it comes added stress. When I was working with Agent Marlow, Hadley took care of Chase and Frankie on some secret Disney film set. No one knew where they were except the production crew. It freaked me out at the time but was absolutely necessary. We couldn't risk the perp having access to any of our family members. It's been a few months since she returned, but she's been nonstop ever since. Maybe it's the nondisclosure agreement she signed on the film or the increased scrutiny from fans and paparazzi. Either way, she's family, and if she needs to bang on my door to have a reprieve, so be it.

"You have to save me," she gushes while fighting to put the pod in the coffee machine. I walk over and take the coffee out of her shaking hands and place it in correctly. I press the button to start the brewing process and turn my attention to a pale-faced Hadley.

"You wanted this career, Hadley. Whatever's happening is okay. You just have to adjust to it, that's all," I say, trying to calm her down.

"Not that, the other thing before that thing became a big thing. Then that thing went somewhere because of the other thing and now I have to attend something to support that thing!" she rambles as she paces in my kitchen. The pot beeps and I'm thankful for the intrusion since I have absolutely no idea what the hell she's talking about.

She continues to dig a trench in my floor as her hands wave wildly about, her eyes darting around but no words coming out of her mouth. I'm at a loss. I never took sign language, and lord knows I don't speak Hadley shorthand, or HSH as my chosen family calls it. Chase seems to be the best interpreter, but he's getting ready for school and I'm in the devil's den.

He tried to teach me their language a bit during the "cool auntie days" but it just flew over my head like rocket science. The two of them became really close during his time on set, and I'm so thankful for it. Those days out with Hadley are sort of like therapy for Chase. They grab pancakes and see horror or action films I would never even consider seeing. She's good for him, but right now, I need her to stop and be an adult for five seconds.

"Hadley!" I yell and hold out her cup of brewed coffee. "Please stop pacing and speak in a language I can understand?"

"Haven't you been listening?" she asks, sipping from her cup.

"You haven't been saying much, just pacing, waving your hands around like you walked through a spider web, and almost killing Frankie's coffee machine," I answer.

She exhales slowly. "I need your help."

"From the thing before the thing." I laugh.

"Exactly!" she answers and plops down at the kitchen table. "Do you have anything to snack on that won't get my trainer pissed at me?"

Since she got back, Hadley's all about being healthy and focusing on what goes into her body. Something about needing to be able to stay healthy on set for long periods of time. Her costar on the film she's currently shooting spread some stomach virus through the cast and crew like the plague. She was the only one who managed to avoid it. It's a bit amusing though, since she meets her trainers in a high-end gym no normal people have access to. She's like a politician with a secret lover. We tease her about it, but secretly we're all thankful she's doing well. Even if it means we don't see her as much.

"So, you'll do it then?" she asks, her eyes looking like a sad puppy's as she pleads with me. I still have no idea what she's asking for. All I know is this is the same look Chase gives me when he wants a new video game or a second scoop of chocolate ice cream.

Before I can answer, the doorbell rings again. I open it to reveal Will in dark blue jeans, a bomber jacket, and his aviator glasses. If I didn't know he had almost died eight months ago, his appearance at my door wouldn't be abnormal. For me, it's a blessing and a curse. I want him back to work with me, but he needs time to heal and recertify.

"Kid ready?" he asks, walking into my now somewhat crowded kitchen. "Cute pj's by the way." I look down at my rainbow unicorn clad pants and shrug.

"Gift from the kid for my birthday. You taking him today?" I ask.

"Yeah, it's career day at school," he answers. He takes off his sunglasses and clips them to the collar of his shirt. "He didn't tell you, did he?"

"Uncle Will, you made it!" Chase rushes into the room, his faded KISS backpack swinging behind him. He stops right in front of the former Marine and salutes. Will returns the gesture before Chase launches himself at Will's legs. "You're even early!"

"Of course, little man. Did you expect anything else from me?" He leans down and pulls Chase into a gentle hug.

My nephew lets go and turns around to face me, his hand firmly in Will's grasp. His radiant smile reminds me of my brother Henry. He's growing up so fast, and his temperament is so much like his parents it's scary. Part of me loves this passage of time, but I dread the battles I know we're going to have. If he's anything at all like the people who brought him into this world, he's going to be taller than me, stubborn as hell, and have a bottomless pit for a stomach.

"Uncle Will is going to Career Day with you?" I ask simply, trying to not sound jealous. I had hoped he would ask me first.

"Yup! He's gonna talk about the Marines and how it's not like video games at all. It's gonna be so cool!" he says excitedly.

"Are you going to spend the whole day or are you coming by the office for some testing?" I ask Will.

"Depends on the kid. Shrink says I'm close to heading back, but you know how they are," he answers.

"Do tell, Will. How are we?" Frankie says from the doorway.

"You're wonderful." Will quickly places his sunglasses back on and smiles at all of us. "It's been a pleasure, ladies, but I really must get this tiny human to school. See you later!"

Chase takes the hint and rushes out of the house, dragging the large muscular Marine with him. I close the door behind the two Keystone Kops before turning my attention back to Hadley. Her leg is bouncing vigorously, her mug is empty, and she's staring into space.

"How long has she been like that?" Frankie asks, her heels clicking against the tiled floor.

"I don't know . . . since she got here? Before Will got here, she was rambling in HSH."

"And you let Chase leave before deciphering?" She smiles at my shrug. "I'm sorry I forgot to tell you. Will's become the big man in his life and he comes with the real-life *Call of Duty* experience," she finishes with air quotes.

"It's fine; as long as the kid is happy, nothing else matters," I say, giving my fiancé a good morning kiss.

"Seriously, can you two not do that all the time?" Hadley pipes up from the table. "Just get married and start being miserable like my parents. This happy stuff is kinda gross."

"She speaks!" Frankie says through laughter. Her engagement ring shimmering in the light still brings a massive smile to my face. After all the bullshit I've put her through, she's still the love of my life. Now if only we could decide on a wedding date, size, and venue, everything would be fine.

As if Frankie can read my mind, she says, "Don't forget to meet me at the venue during lunch, okay?" She grabs her keys from the hook and stands by the door. She pulls me in for another kiss and a tight hug. "If we finish early, we can get lunch together." Her breath feels so hot on the skin directly below my ear that my brain stops functioning. My knees shake and my hands tighten into fists behind her back. She knows exactly what's she's doing. I love it.

"You're coming, right?" Hadley's voice barely registers in my ears.

"I wish," Frankie mumbles with a suggestive grin.

"Yup," I say breathlessly.

Hadley jumps up from her chair, causing Frankie and I to jump apart. "Excellent! I'll make sure you two are on the guest list for the premiere. It'll have some Q&A after, red carpet and all that crap. So, come prepared!" She gives Frankie a quick hug before turning to me. "You are a lifesaver." She kisses me on my cheek before exiting my house.

"What the hell did we just agree to?" I ask Frankie.

"A red-carpet movie premiere, apparently," she answers with a smile. "Oh, before I forget, my father and brothers are coming to visit. They want to discuss the wedding. Love you." She closes the door quickly behind her. I suddenly have the urge to throw up.

Upstairs my cell phone rings, and I rush back into the bedroom to grab it.

"Steele?" I answer slightly out of breath.

"I know you had plans today, but I'm sending Sydney to pick you up. We might have another Carnation Killer case or a copycat. Either way, clear your plate until further notice," Zeile says.

"Yes, sir," I answer and quickly hanging up. The tension in my shoulders builds as I think about the cold case file sitting in my desk drawer. The one I spoke about only a day ago. It's moments like this where you pray it isn't a copycat so you can catch them in a mistake. Then you feel guilty because someone else had to die for you to find it. No one ever wins.

***

Exiting the elevator, several officers pass us in the hallway. Captain Zeile waits by the hotel room door. The drive out of our jurisdiction was annoying with traffic, and we were unable to move regardless of the sirens. Nature of the beast during the morning rush hour.

"Sir?"

"Body's inside. Dr. Hayes is already in there with the crime scene unit. Photos were already taken to preserve the crime scene, but we needed to get a jump on this fast," he answers.

"If the victim was pronounced, normally no one should go in before detectives do," I say a bit defiantly. This is the first major case he's overseeing me, so we need to get on the same page.

"New order, Steele. I'm personally involved in every case that needs it." He pulls his shoulders back and stands taller than before.

"This is out of our jurisdiction. Even if it is our cold case, the locals have control over this section," I say. The unfamiliar faces of two detectives in the hallway turn my way. Their expressions are full of frustration and borderline anger.

"New protocol from One PP," he says as if that explains everything. "I'll see you back at the office." He turns and walks down the hallway, away from the scene.

"Now that he's gone, we're going in," the younger, more fit, and dis-gruntled detective says. A uniformed officer holds up his hand, prevent-ing him from entering the scene.

"I'm sorry, but we've got specific orders from Captain Zeile. No one in or out that hasn't been approved," the middle-aged cop blandly recites.

"Just let us in. It's our district and our body, which means it's our case," the second detective with a sorry attempt for facial hair says.

"And I'm one year away from my twenty. I don't give a shit about you and your case. I just keep my head down, do what I'm told, and retire with a full pension."

"Excuse me," Sydney says to the men as she flashes her badge. "I believe we're on the list."

"Well shit, Steele. You got a new partner since you almost got your last one killed? Another case of numbers, right? Gotta keep up with equality! Then again, maybe it's for the best. She dies, the department doesn't lose much," the second detective continues.

I see Sydney's face harden and I do my best to push her a bit behind me. I'm the senior detective, and it's my job to protect her. I flip open my badge for the officer at the door to scan. He nods and waves us in. The chubby detective with the scruff of facial hair grabs my arm harshly and I turn to meet his eyes.

"Look, Steele." I turn to him, shocked he knows my name. "Everyone knows who you are. The token dyke for NYPD equality. Maybe that's why you got away with all the bullshit with the Garrison case. Either way, when this all calms down, you'll be remembered as the bitch who stole what's ours."

I yank my arm free of his grasp and step into his personal space. "I don't give a fuck what you think of me, but a person is dead. If this is all about case numbers, feel free to take it. This killer's been sitting in my drawer for years. It'll fuck with your padded stats. Now get out of my face."

The two of them back off slowly, as if that would somehow intimidate me more. I watch them until they're out of sight. The uniformed officer stands calmly to the side, pretending he didn't hear anything.

"You okay?" Sydney asks.

"Nothing I haven't faced before. You?" I ask.

"Same." Her eyes remain focused on the empty hallway. If looks could kill, those two would be burned to a crisp.

"Thankfully not everyone is like him, right?" I say to the officer at the door.

"Just getting my twenty, ma'am," he says, dismissing me. Nope, like at every other job in America, there are those who just want to get paid and others who live quietly under the patriarchal bullshit. Either way, no one wants to rock the boat that they're standing in, regardless of the negative effects their lack of action causes.

Walking into the hotel room, I see Medical Examiner Victor Hayes by the body. There are only two other people in the room. There are usually more CSI team members in here covering every possible surface with fingerprint dust. Victor notices me scanning the area.

"I kicked them out," he says from near the bed. I walk over to him and give him a questioning glare. "The other CSIs. Told them more than two would mess with the evidence we have. Namely our Jane Doe here."

Her body is white, almost ghastly pale. Blood from the cuts on her chest has rolled down below her breast and dried, staining the sheets. "He didn't clean her up." I look over to Sydney to see that she's taking notes. She's already on it.

"Maybe he was in a rush," she suggests.

"Maybe, or maybe it isn't him," I respond.

"Or they just didn't wait for her body to hit full rigor or for the blood to clot. I'm pretty sure it's the same person," Victor says. He holds up a swab from the body. "I normally wait until we're back at the lab, but I swabbed her vaginal canal just in case. Smells like . . . you know."

It is him. Or her. Whoever it is has decided to come out of hiding and kill again.

"Excuse me?" Sydney asks quietly.

"I'll explain later. Just write the smell is consistent with previous cases, please," I say, trying to calm the roil of acid in my empty stomach. That's the last thing I need right now. "Do we have any idea who she is?"

"Not currently," one of the CSIs answers. "Luggage tags were removed. Wallet is missing." We're taking everything to the lab. Once Dr. Hayes removes the body, we'll check the rest of the room for any particulates."

"Thorough, but it's going to bury you under a lot of needless evidence. No one cleans as well as they say," I toss back. "Vic, I need whatever you can as soon as you can."

Two men walk in with a long, black bag. The sound of the zipper opening makes the hair on my neck stand up. Death comes for us all in the end, but it doesn't make it any easier to accept. Two sets of gloved hands lift Jane Doe's body up and place her in the bag. The zipping sound hits me once again before the two men lift the bag up and carry the victim out of the room and toward the waiting gurney in the hallway.

"I'll get what I can to you as soon as possible," Victor says as he heads out of the room.

"Hey, Vic?" He turns. "Priority one," I say simply. He nods in understanding and walks out of view.

I kneel by the bed, looking over the crumbled-up sheets. The victim was naked and left on the bed for us to find. "You have a light?" I ask one of the CSIs as I point to the bed. He hands me a long bar ultraviolet light. Clicking it on reveals what appear to be semen stains. "We'll need the sheets," I say as I click the light off.

Nothing else in the room looks overly disturbed. It looks used, as it should. This is the standard modus operandi. It's frustrating walking around the room, taking in the commonness of it all. The bathroom is much of the same. Toiletries laid out on the sink. Tub dry, clean. Shower drain might hold something, but once again, nothing seems to stand out.

Walking back into the bedroom, I watch Sydney as she snaps photos of the scene on her cell phone. She walks around the room, getting what seems to be awkward angles for images.

"What do you see?" I ask her.

"Just trying to get into the mind of the killer. I find photos from their point of view helps me recreate the crime in my head," she says, putting her phone back in her blazer. "Other than that, everything is too . . ."

"Normal."

"Exactly."

I watch Sydney walk around the crime scene, taking it all in. No blood splatter on the walls, no evidence of a fight anywhere. This is going to be another notch on the Carnation Killer's belt. Another torment on mine.

***

An hour later we pull up to Woodlake Public Cemetery. I ignore the confused look on Sydney's face as I exit the car. I walk along the grass, following the line of headstones, all purchased at one point in time in preparation of the afterlife, or just the housing of your corpse. I hear the door close behind me, followed by muttering as Sydney's heels sink into the dirt.

"Mind telling me why we're here?" she asks.

I continue walking until I come across a headstone I know all too well. The carved letters of Reyna Lewis stare back at me, the stone weathered from years of local storms, pollution, and whatever else Mother Nature sticks to it.

"Her best friend had her buried here. Reyna had no family, just her friends and a dog. Eve insisted that she would love being this close to the city for eternity. Apparently, the two of them had been traveling together since college. Eve hasn't been back since Reyna's murder." The wind blows, sending a chill up my spine. I shove my hands into my pants pockets, but my eyes remain firmly on the grave.

"Why'd you bring me here?"

"Reyna was just a normal woman enjoying a weekend away, living her life. Then someone decides she's the one to die. It's a reality that too many detectives forget. The job helps desensitize every compassionate fiber in your being with time," I say softly.

"You wouldn't be here if it had," Sydney replies almost defiantly.

"My family is a few rows over. I used to go there all the time. It reminded me there was something unfinished."

"The Garrison case."

"Yeah, that little obsession of mine."

"Now you come here instead. You've switched one for another."

"There's going to be more detectives like the one today. The ones who want to bring you down because of your orientation, the color of your skin, or because you prefer heels. You have to find something, anything, to bring you back to why you do this." I kneel down and pull out a small weed by the headstone. "For me, it's closure for the families. Garrison was mine; the Keets family deserves it as well. We can't forget the reason we have a job—to catch the individual out there who decided to harm an innocent person."

"And if they're not innocent?" she counters.

I trace the lines of Reyna's name, committing the feel to memory once again. Sydney stands behind me, and I can feel her eyes boring into the back of my head. Once I'm finished, I stand up and fix my jacket.

"No one deserves violence thrust upon them," I answer simply.

"Some criminals do," she answers. She turns to walk away, but I grab her forearm and stop her.

"I don't care who has done what. No one deserves to be violated."

She turns, walks into my space, and stops directly in front of me. Her brown eyes harden as she tilts her head up to stare me down.

"You did everything you could to bring down your boogeyman. Don't go high and mighty now, detective. Lying doesn't suit you." She turns and walks away. Her heels slip on the turf, and she curses under her breath.

I follow her to the car, and several thoughts rush through my mind. A drop of rain hits my jacket and pulls my attention. The wet stain spreads like a virus until another one hits. Then another. My pace quickens as the raindrops are now so thick you can see them. I slip into the driver's side of the car as the sky pours down on us. Sydney stares out the window, looking at the rows of memories lost.

"You're right. I might not have broken any laws, and I did everything that I could to bring him down. I didn't think about the people I lost. Hell, I almost lost my life, and for what? To bring down an asshole and his family," I say. Sydney continues to stare out the window, so I continue. "It didn't help me deal with the issues at home. I still had a kid to raise, a heart to win back, friendships to repair."

"What's your point, Steele?" she asks sharply.

"I let it consume me. So, yeah, I'm a fucking hypocrite to a point. I also go to a shitload of therapy and have decided to keep my integrity. It's all we have in this job. I saw you at the scene. If those two fools started a fight, you would have finished it," I say.

"You have no idea what it's like. You can hide your dyke side. I can't hide my skin color," she says, instantly regretting her choice of words. "I didn't mean . . ."

"Yes, you did. It's all good. And you're right. Theoretically, I can. Sadly, it doesn't work when my fiancée is one of our forensic psychologists." I lean back in the seat and snap my seatbelt in place before cranking the car. "This case has haunted me since Reyna died. She was the third victim."

"Why are you telling me this?"

"Until further notice, you're stuck being my partner. That means your needs are mine and vice versa. Keets is your obsession. Carnation asshole is my current one. Deal?"

She turns to face me, her face calmer than before. She nods her head and that's all the affirmation I need. I begin to drive through the blinding rain back to the precinct.

"That being said, you have any advice for someone seeing her soon-to-be-in-laws this weekend?" I say, changing the subject.

"Don't drink before you meet them, and if you go out, don't order fish. Ever." She laughs, and I feel the tension in the car dissipate instantly.

I know I didn't need to bring her here. It was for me to get my points across. Maybe I made them, maybe I didn't. I just know we're on the same page, working as a team until the boss says otherwise. That's all I wanted.

***

Walking in the front door, I place my keys on the small table before dropping down on the bench by the door. I can faintly hear Chase yelling at something upstairs in his room. Probably a multi-player shooter game or something similar. Frankie's hushed voice emanates from the kitchen. I kick my shoes off and head that way. Maybe pizza and old episodes of our favorite show will wash away today. When I'm about two steps from the room, Frankie's tone shifts, and her decibel level increases. Not to the point of yelling, but where she is crystal clear to whomever she's talking to.

"I know you're upset, but I expect you to be nice." She pauses, and I swear I can hear the eye roll or huff of discontent. "Waylon, I don't care. This is what I want. You, Dad, and Wade need to respect that."

Leaning on the wall just out of view, I tap my head gently against the sheetrock. Frankie's family were never fans of mine. I was always the kid with big dreams and little to show for it. When I went into the academy, I thought they would somehow be more accepting of her dating me. The discontent shifted from money to not coming home after one of my shifts.

When we separated, Frankie talked to her middle brother Waylon. He was her partner in crime growing up, so her leaning on him was a natural part of our breakup. It turned out to be a blessing that she hadn't told her older brother Wade or her father for a couple of months. Hadley assumed it was her way of hoping we'd get back together. I always felt it was her embarrassment at what happened. Our epic failure.

Either way, I was very thankful Wade was not privy to any information that gave him an excuse to come to New York and bury me in an endzone somewhere. He's a part-time high school football coach, so when I asked for permission to marry Frankie, he threatened to hide my body under the goalposts. At least he was more creative than her dad. He just told me he had a shotgun and knew how to use it. Maybe they'd end my existence as a team.

When we decided to try again, I knew her family was unhappy. I'm sure her father, and Wade wanted her to find a stable, loving gentleman to make her happy. Her dad was never in our faces about his displeasure for her preference, but when it came up, he spoke about his dreams for her future being dashed. So, when she accepted my proposal, Mr. Ryan was a bit miffed at the whole thing. First, it was me all over again. Second, I didn't ask his permission this time. I didn't know there was an expiration date on things like this, but apparently, I stepped outside the lines and incurred an offsides call with about sixty-yard penalty or something like that.

"Dad, please stop this," Frankie continues, her voice strained with emotion. "I love her. I love Chase, He's as close to a grandson . . ." I hear her take a deep breath. "I understand. I'll see you when you're in town."

She drops the phone on the table, and it's then I make my presence known. She looks up at me, her eyes full of unshed tears, her face blank, and her body slumped in a way I don't see often. She looks beaten.

"How much did you hear?" she asks softly as a few tears fall.

"Only your side, but a little." I walk in and sit next to her. I take both her hands in mine, the engagement ring scraping the inside of my palm with the pressure. "What happened?"

"They don't approve," she says and laughs sarcastically. "My brothers don't want me to marry someone who left me. . ." She swallows hard. "What did I ever do to make him hate me so much?" She finally breaks.

"He doesn't hate you, Frankie. He's angry at me. And because he couldn't protect you from what I did," I say, trying to calm her. "Can you blame them? All of them wanted you to be happy, and then I fucked it all up. It's natural for them to be leery of anything I say or do." My lips press against our joined hands.

"It's not up to them, Jasmine." She pulls her hand away and lifts my chin to meet my gaze. "We hurt each other. End of story. Full stop. I can't keep going back there. We're moving forward and getting married. Chase is going to be our ring bearer . . ."

"Or best man." I chuckle lightly.

"I think Victor might be upset with that," Frankie responds with a smile. "Point is, this is about us. They're either in or they're not. I can't let them live my life. It's you and I versus the world. For forever and a day."

"Always and forever," I reply simply. "When do they come in?"

"They're coming in this Friday and fly out Tuesday."

"You want Chase to be here? I'm sure I can talk to Will and see if he can take him for a boy's weekend," I offer.

"I'd love that, but I'd also like Chase and all our friends to be around. I don't want to walk on eggshells this time. I want my family to see my life . . . my real existence. Not something I cater to them. I can't do that anymore."

"I don't want you to ever again," I say, leaning closer to her.

Frankie reaches around my neck and buries her hands in my long, brown hair. Her nails scratch gently on my scalp, and I find myself pulling her onto my lap. Her skirt riding up slightly, my hands resting on her bare thighs. Her breath hits my nose, and my heart rate increases exponentially. Frankie's lips graze mine as my hands pull her body firmly against me. I kiss her hard, showering her with all the confidence and love I can.

"Parental units, I'm hungry," Chase says, turning the corner into the kitchen. "Ewww! Oh my God, my eyes!" he screams, rubbing his eyes as he rushes back into the living room.

Frankie lifts herself off my lap and kisses my nose. "I'll go find out what the darling child wants to eat for dinner. I have a feeling a call to the pizza place will be happening."

"I'm blind, Mama! How can I play video games if I'm blind?" Chase continues his antics from the other room.

We both stop dead. Chase has never called either of us anything other than aunt. This is a new development.

"Good luck with that one," I say, trying to defuse the tension.

"He's got your family genetics, just remember that," she answers.

"He's biologically related to me. I can't fix that. You *chose* to adopt him," I say.

"My lord, you two are so alike he might as well be your son!" she tosses at me walking out of the room.

My son . . . I like the sound of that. I wish my brother was still here, but him giving me Chase was the greatest gift I could ever ask for. He helped me understand unconditional love. He gave me a family I never knew I needed. He gave me a reason to keep fighting.

Chapter Three

It's four a.m., and for the first time in a long time, I'm not the only person in my office at this ungodly hour. Most detectives don't keep normal hours anyway, but with Will out until he can pass all of his recertifications, it's unusual to have company. Me, myself, and I are alone for most days. Today though, Sydney is sitting in Will's chair. Boxes litter what was once my organized and clean office.

"Morning, Steele," she says without looking up. "I got you a peppermint tea." She looks up at me. "Captain said you can't have coffee."

"It's an acid reflux thing, not a 'dying-on-the-side-of-the-road' thing," I grumble.

I step over the boxes, drape my leather jacket over the back of my chair, and grab the tea off the desk. It smells heavenly, but it's hot as hell when I take a sip, and I cringe in pain as the fluid scorches my esophagus.

"It's hot."

"No shit."

"Don't go spitting that all over the case files," she says as she gets up from Will's desk.

"You got all the case files released to us? Already?" I don't mask my astonishment.

"Captain fast-tracked it. Feels like strings were pulled at the highest level," Sydney says with a slight uptick in her voice.

"New captain, new response time, I guess," I say. I pick up the box closest to my feet and drop it on my desk.

"Or our necks are gonna be on the line with this one," Sydney replies.

"They always are, Sydney." I toss the top of the evidence box to the floor. "One thing's for sure: we're starting from square one here. We're going to have to reinterview, revisit, whatever to figure this out. I don't think the powers that be will accept another body dropped on the department."

Sydney grabs the box closest to her and places it on her desk, flips open the top, and pulls out the files. She pushes evidence bags around before looking at a piece of paper in the box.

"Some of the evidence was destroyed in this one." She holds up a wrinkled piece of paper. "Looks like water damage." She looks in the box and moves some bags around. "The evidence bags might be fine, but the paperwork is going to be difficult to read."

"I'm sure we can get the important details. It's the detective's notes I'd be more concerned about," I answer as I continue to flip through the papers in another file.

"You weren't the lead on this?"

"Nope, my old partner Gino Reyes was," I say, my voice thick with regret. "We're going to need to go through everything, maybe recreate the crime scenes based on the photos and interview people again."

"Let me get the main files out. We'll set up a timeline on the board," she says and reads a name from a file. "Detective Reyes caught the case with the first victim: Olivia Anders."

"Yeah. Good guy . . . career killing case."

She stands and walks over to the dry erase boards, grabs a marker, and writes the first victim's name on the top and underlines it. "Found in the back of an abandoned van in the Bronx." She pauses and flips through the pages. "That can't be right."

"It is," I say. "Mrs. Anders was a wife and mother of two from Syracuse, New York. Her husband Nick had to drive down and identify the body."

"What is a White, middle-aged woman doing in the back of a van in the Bronx?" Sydney adds incredulously.

"Being murdered apparently."

"You know what I mean," she replies sharply.

"I do. No drugs in her system. No affair. Was down in the city for some me time at a high-end spa. Alcohol was well over the legal limit, so Reyes assumed she was unconscious during . . . everything."

"I don't know any woman who would want to go to New York City alone for a spa weekend."

"She had a ticket to see Hamilton in her luggage."

"Okay, now *that* is a reason to come to the city," Sydney says with a slight smirk.

"Nick said his wife loved coming to the city alone for a weekend every now and again. She would see a show, have some spa treatments, and go home. Apparently, when her daughter was old enough, she planned on bringing her along. Simple, boring family." I lean on my desk near Sydney.

"So, what was so special about her?" She flips through the crime scene photos. "One white carnation, heart carved into her skin by the petals . . . and cleaned?"

"Clorox-based cleaning solution. He wiped down the whole body, flushed her vaginal canal to kill any and all DNA. Reports state the hearts are carved after she's cleaned. Makes logical sense," I recite from memory.

"Are all of them like this?"

"Different races, religions, social circles, ages . . . you name it. No real trail."

"Can you trace the flowers?"

"Generic white carnations? Every place in the city sells them. The shops closest to the crime scenes hadn't sold any during the time frame of the murder. It's gotta be part of the kit he carries around. That being said, we can't canvas every single flower shop in the five boroughs and Long Island."

"Long Island?"

"Elizabeth Cook, found in her apartment in Westbury. Nassau County kicked it back to the city since she was victim number four."

"You get a lot of that, huh?" She looks over at my obvious confusion and holds her hands up in mock surrender. "The Garrison case. There was a body in a cooler in Nassau County. Cops handed it to you."

"Trust me, if Cook were the first victim, I would have given everything over to them. Not because I'm an asshole, but maybe the case might have turned out differently." Sydney continues reading files notes and writing on the whiteboard.

"You think they would have solved it before more victims were found?"

"That's the thing, I don't know. I just remember my old partner Gino Reyes making me work every possible corner, angle, forensic evidence runs . . . You name it, he made me run it. It just felt like we missed everything. Like we are always two steps behind the killer rather than ahead of him. I have watched this case eat away at everyone who touches it."

"Hasn't killed you," Sydney comments, staring at the board.

"I wasn't the lead investigator. After Reyes . . . retired, they pawned it off on some other detective. I was still too new for them to trust me with it. So, I focused on my own demons. For better or for worse." I stand next to her, looking over the whiteboard. "And now, you're here with me, staring at this board of information hoping we can figure this out before number six."

"Shit's gonna hit the fan if we don't. I heard the captain telling you people are watching your every move. Media and right wingers love a shit show." She crosses her arms and surveys the board.

"Probably." I remain silent for a few seconds. "Cook always seemed like an extraneous variable. An outlier if you will. Everything else was in the metropolitan area. So, the question is: If her death was a mistake, why was he away from his normal haunts?"

"Until we find some kind of pattern, we won't know for sure."

"I say we hit the forensics first. Let me introduce you to Dr. Brown and beg her to retest everything we have in these boxes. Maybe her team can find something to put us on track."

***

Exiting the elevator to the forensics lab, I show my ID to the woman sitting at the desk before I sign in. Sydney follows suit before we walk through the glass doors into the pristine, overly white labs. We're in a section of Manhattan where dirt with anything is a major color combination, in an unassuming brick precinct building, and we have two major labs that would make any science fiction fan geek out.

"The whole point of a vacation is to get away from all of this," I hear Dr. Lillian Brown say through the glass doors. "I understand that, Victor, but you promised me Hawaii for a romantic getaway and now you're offering me Montauk in the middle of winter!"

The back of her chair moves as she shifts from one side to the other. I know she had started seeing Vic outside of work, but I wasn't aware they had progressed to romantic getaway status. Maybe I should sit my friend down and explain to him the meaning of romance . . . or commitment. He seems to be struggling with that since his divorce was finalized.

"I understand work is important, but it doesn't come first. Figure out the dates and we are going to Hawaii so I can lay out on the beach."

The chair spins around and her face twists into a face my mother used when I was in serious trouble. "I know I don't like the sun, but that doesn't mean my ass doesn't want to be drinking a mai tai while relaxing on a fucking beach!" She slams the phone down and rubs her eyes. After what feels like an uncomfortable eternity, I knock gently on the glass doors. Lillian looks up, blushes, and smirks before pushing a button to open the doors.

"How much did you hear?" she asks.

"It's got to be nice having doors only you can open, but wow, that sound carries through. Mai tais?" I answer sarcastically.

"You're an ass."

"Not usually. I'm more of an ignorant oaf and someone who uses humor when she's truly uncomfortable, so yup, that's me."

"I'm Detective Sydney Locke," Sydney says and extends her hand.

"Where are my manners?" Lillian stands and takes hold of Sydney's outstretched hand. "Dr. Lillian Brown."

"If there's a scrap of evidence, this one will find it, so make sure you hide anything you don't want her to analyze," I say.

"You're fidgeting. What's wrong, Jasmine?" Lillian asks me.

"Nothing," I add quickly.

"Is this about the bachelorette party Hadley and I are planning for Frankie?" She folds her arms.

"No, why would it be? I mean, you're all going to go out and spend lots of money on drinks, and do fun things to celebrate, and I won't—"

Lillian cuts me off. "You're babbling. Just stop thinking about it. Frankie is going to have a good time before walking down the aisle. That's all I'm going to say. It's a surprise, and we both know you and keeping secrets don't go hand in hand."

"Okay." I flop into a seat across from her desk. "That's not what we're here about."

"I assumed as much." Lillian walks around her desk and sits down. She motions for Sydney to sit next to me. "What can I do for you?"

"Redo all testing from the Carnation Killer's case files?" Sydney blurts out quickly.

Lillian leans back in her chair and laughs a bit at the absurdity of the request. She looks between Sydney and me a few times before leaning forward again. She types frantically on her keyboard.

"All the information is in the database; I don't see a reason to retest."

"With all due respect to the previous doc who handled this, we need fresh eyes. You weren't here when the other victims came in. You'll be getting the evidence to test from the most recent one. In order to do a proper analysis, you should understand the previous files to compare them to," I state, sounding like a former professor of mine.

"You sell it well, but I could easily read the information from the file for comparison," she counters.

"But you might notice something from the other files that was missed. Detective Steele has been working on this case since the early stages. I've only come onboard recently, so I'm catching up. It would really help us if you could start from scratch with me," Sydney pleads.

"She's good." Lillian eyes me as she leans back in her chair. "Did your mother teach you how to manipulate people with your words?" she says to Sydney.

"No," Sydney says with a bit of defiance in her voice. The two women stare each other down until Lillian's hard exterior breaks and she smirks. "My uncle. He could con you out of anything in your closet or bank account."

"How many marriages?" Lillian pries deeper.

"Five marriages, one failed engagement, and several loves of his life," Sydney says without emotion. "The only person he ever loved more than himself was his reflection."

Lillian breaks out into sincere laughter. She leans forward and looks over some papers on her desk. "If you have a deadline, I can't promise we'll make it. Victor should be sending up the new samples, and those are the priority. That being said, I think I can try and make sure all extra personnel are working on retesting everything from those previous cases." When Lillian lays on professionalism heavy, she reminds me of my father in teacher mode.

"No deadlines, Lil. Just do the best you can as soon as humanly possible. Hell, maybe we got lucky and he made a mistake this time," I answer as I stand up.

"The probability of that would be slim to . . ." Sydney stops talking as she sees the look of disbelief on my face. "Sorry, I just state facts randomly sometimes."

"Great, I'm working with a human Wikipedia page," I mumble, turning toward Lillian. "Let me know when you have anything or need anything or whatever. Okay?"

She waves her hand to dismiss us as she turns the volume up on a Herbie Hancock song emanating from her computer speakers. I hold the door open for Sydney and follow her out.

"Where to now?" she asks.

"Well, now we go back to the office and continue breaking down the timeline while we shove unhealthy burgers and fries down our throats," I say a little happier than I intend as I walk down the hall away from her.

"Couldn't we get a salad or something a bit . . . smarter?" she asks.

"We could, but that would make me really unhappy. Stressful times call for bad, fatty foods."

"But—"

"Food, Locke, my treat. Then we're gonna go through the rest of those boxes when I get back."

I step into the elevator and smile at her confusion. Sometimes you have to take a step back and breathe before you move forward. It's something I adopted from Captain Tyler Udall. There are days I miss my old captain and replay his funeral over and over again in my mind. *One smart step at a time, no more going it alone.* I grab my wallet from my back pocket, flip it open, and stare at a miniature replica pin of Tyler's badge. My fingers graze the outline of it. His wife gave it to me after the funeral as a reminder. We always have each other's backs but demand the best as well. We're never alone.

The whiteboard has information scattered all over it. My bacon burger and fries sit half-eaten on my desk, while Sydney's was gone a long time ago. Looking at the stack of minutia on my desk, I can feel the tension in my neck growing. Beyond this case there's another stack of papers waiting to be filed, signed, and organized. And then there's all the reports I'm letting lapse. That's the one side of the job that no one likes: paperwork.

"If I stare at this any longer, I swear to God my eyes are going to bleed," I say, rubbing my eyes.

"We've been at it for hours, and I can't see any pattern at all. Is it possible that he's truly random?" Sydney asks before gulping down some of her Diet Coke.

"The one thing I've learned between school, cases, and various true crime series that I've binge-watched is there's no such thing as random. Everything has a point, a purpose, or a connection of some kind." I stand up and walk to the board.

"All different women, different ages, no apparent connection in any way as to location or work or school . . . I have no fucking clue how this son of a bitch finds these women," Sydney says.

"The problem we have right now is that we're faced with half the equation. We only have what he leaves behind," I say absentmindedly.

"That's usually what we deal with, Steele. It's not like we can just call him in and have a full conversation or judicial hearing."

"I understand that, but maybe there is a pattern but we don't have all the pieces of the puzzle to put it together. There has to be something—maybe an internet search history, school history . . . anything that can lead us to whomever this person is. I'm praying it's in the forensics or that something falls into our lap because at this point"—I toss my unfinished food in the trash—"it's only a matter of time before we have another victim on our hands."

"Where are you going?" she asks.

"I think we need to stop for the day. Victor's still working on the newest body. Lillian is going through all the evidence from the current case and all the previous ones. At this point, we're in a holding pattern. What else can we do except bang our heads against the table and pray the blood leaves us a line from point A to point B? We need sleep, and we need to look at this with fresh eyes in the morning. Maybe something triggers me when I get home. it's happened to me before."

"Would you mind if I stay here a little while longer and continue going through everything?" She's staring at the picture of the newest victim in front of her.

"Just don't stay too late. I don't need to worry about you getting home in one piece." I grab my jacket and put it on as my cell phone beeps with the message. "Looks like Victor's having trouble with the identification. He says he needed to request security clearance."

"That's not a good thing for us, is it?"

"Depends. Could work in our favor, or it can blow up in our faces and we'll have the entire Police Department or government breathing down our necks. Hell, if that's the case, they might take it away from us," I say pulling open the office door.

"Would that be such a bad thing? They have more resources and you've worked with the FBI before."

"The one thing you'll learn about the government — and this department — is that they're both the good old boys club. They've got great intentions, but they lack the finesse that some of these cases require. It's not for lack of trying; it's just the way they've been raised and trained. I got lucky with Agent Marlow. Anyone else would've stepped on my toes, ignored my team, and taken full control without having taken one step in my shoes," I say before leaving the office, closing the door behind me.

Since the end of the Garrison case, there's been a spotlight on my precinct and the NYPD for their assistance with the Seattle branch of the FBI. There's also been increased scrutiny on everything that has my name attached to it. There were a few lawyers who combed through every case my hands ever touched just looking for a reason for a retrial. Hell, they even came up with what they called the *Steele Defense*. They claimed I had a personal vendetta and used extreme measures and some other bullshit. I stopped listening when they claimed I had the scientific means, the motive, and the access to change their client's DNA sample that was found within the body of the woman he killed. I might be a bitch, but I still need my nephew's help to set up anything on my cell phone, Wi-Fi, Xbox, you name it. I don't think it's in my repertoire to change DNA. I'm no Barbara McClintock.

Not like attorneys don't use everything they can to get you to slip up. They are there for one reason and one reason only: acquittal or, worst case, leniency in sentencing. In one of the first cases I testified for, a perp tried to prove this lowly beat cop had it in for him. His lawyer went on the attack, ripping me apart for my connections to the accused. He spoke of my many visits to Riker's Island which were all recorded and documented by the case file.

The fact that I was a secondary officer to the DA as protection was omitted. Not precisely a lie, but not quite the proper setting either. I remember the Drakkar-wearing guy with the cheap suit and sideburns from the seventies leaning over the edge of the witness booth trying to intimidate me. He spoke about me being a new officer in my uniform with crisp polyester khakis and how I wanted people to respect me. I spoke in facts as my training officer taught me. Routine stop, eyes were bloodshot, jittery—all the signs of something being off. Enough to insist on a sobriety test, which the driver refused.

Jerry, my training officer, took the lead since I was so green and unsure of the next steps. I remember his eyes kept darting to the trunk of the old white Pontiac with rust spots everywhere. The Dalmatian-looking car housed more than we could have imagined. Once Jerry opened the trunk, the guy took off in the other direction.

The guy's wife was bound and bloodied. Her injuries were pretty severe, but her eyes are what stuck with me to this day. The fear in them was like nothing I had seen before. Sadly, I've seen the look many times over since then. People in situations out of their control all show the same fear. It doesn't matter their color or religion; it's all the same torment.

I remember the lawyer just ignored everything I said and immediately asked why I kept staring at his client during the trial. I was trying to figure out what turns a human being into such a vile individual. Blame my degree, but my brain couldn't process why a person could do those horrible things to a woman he loved. Needless to say, they attacked me harder, stating I tried to use my newfound authority to seduce the assailant. He rejected me and I created this unfounded anger to get revenge. It didn't matter that another officer testified in line with me or that the hospital showcased her injuries; the suggestion of my impropriety was getting questionable glances.

There are a few moments in my career that have brought a smile to my face. When the defense attorney asked me an inane question, I remember being calm while I stated I had no desire to lay with a man, let alone his client. When he prodded me further, I informed him I was gay and dating a lovely woman. I don't know which expression was more priceless, his or his clients. They tried to change tactics, but the jury wanted nothing to do with it. He went away for a long time. Just proves that a defense team will come up with anything to get their client off. Sadly, innocent people get caught up in this desperation from a guilty individual.

That fraudulent defense case aside, the news media ran wild with how we had managed to take down a large corruption ring. Some of them went into full detail of the case and the victims involved. Others found a way to twist it and use it to drum up fear in their fan base. We even had some senators from Washington demanding we provide them with any and all information about the illegal immigrants that were granted asylum. They missed the point completely. Women were raped, tortured, and beaten. It took a hell of a lot of courage for them to speak up against their assailants. Like I said: the good old boys lack finesse.

Chapter Four

W armth surrounds me on this Friday morning. A weekend with dinners, festivals, and whatever gets lumped into my schedule is just around the corner. Frankie's small frame wrapped around me, her soft snoring in my ear, is the most beautiful way to wake up.

"What's going on in that mind of yours?" she mumbles, half awake.

"Nothing much. Just enjoying this moment," I reply, my voice low.

Her arms quickly release me, my back hits the bed, and Frankie stares down at me. She looks concerned, her hand on my face as she rests on her left forearm.

"What's wrong?"

"We're not sleeping?" I toss out quickly. Her defiant face forces the next sarcastic comment out of my mouth to fade away into the ether. "Your family comes in today, and I have this case to focus on. If her father, Wade, and Waylon didn't dislike me before, they will now. I can't just walk out of work to—"

Her lips press against mine, silencing me. As I pull her gently on top of me, one leg falls between mine and her hands find purchase in my hair. It's a dance we've always managed to perform to a pleasurable perfection.

"Aunt Jazz!"

At least we did before the tiny human lived in this house. Her head hits my chest as our breathing levels out.

"He's going to be with Will for most of the weekend. As for my family, let me handle them. I took a few days off to show them around the city."

"Lose them in Central Park and come home for an afternoon delight?" I ask with a smile on my face. She raises her head and smacks my arm.

"You have a one-track mind!"

"Do you blame me?" I kiss her nose. "You're stunning."

"Mama!" Chase screams up the stairs. "I can't reach the cereal."

"She'll will be right down!" I call back to Chase.

Frankie shakes her head and slowly pulls herself out of bed. The short T-shirt she borrowed from me falls off her shoulder, revealing her one and only tattoo. A simple tiger, crawling his way up her skin. It begs for attention, but I force myself to stay put.

"I moved the cereal to the bottom shelf so he could feed himself in the morning."

"And I moved it back to the top one. I want him to eat healthier options, not sugar and genetically engineered chemical food."

"Hey, don't attack my Lucky Charms like that! They got me through college and are the snack of champions. Not to mention, they're magically delicious!"

"What? It's the favorite food of diabetics everywhere. I got you off coffee, I can get the kid to eat oatmeal every other day."

"Oh my God, you have become my mother. If you take away my chocolate addiction, I will hide your Broadway musical collection!" I say.

"It's in iTunes," she counters.

"I'll change your password and give you nothing but Nickelback, Vanilla Ice, and other obscure random songs that will irritate you forever." I sit up and smile.

She crawls to me and kisses me hard on the lips. My body instantly responds to her touch and soft moan of desire.

"Do that and you'll never see my birthmark again." She kisses me softly again before walking out of the room.

"You wouldn't do that!" I yell after her. The laughter greeting my ears makes my heart fall for her even more. It's a blessing to have this relationship, for better or worse, growing together as one.

My cell phone vibrates against the wood nightstand, and the image of my favorite metrosexual stares at me with a smirk. Victor calling before his normal working hours has notoriously been a bad sign.

"Vic," I manage to get out.

"We have a serious problem, Jazz. You better get here, like now," he stammers before hanging up the phone. My head hits the headboard hard. It's not going to be a good day. Fuck, it's not going to be a good *weekend*.

The first thing that hits me as I walk into the precinct is the gaggle of men dressed in fatigues talking to my boss. Two of them are higher in rank based on the number of stripes on their lapels. The rest seem like a supporting cast of characters for a show of strength rather than necessity. Holding my peppermint tea in one hand and my office key in the other, I move through the crowd, trying to reach the security of my office.

"Steele." Zeile's voice rings over the noise in the pen, stopping me in my tracks. My well-worn boots squeak on the gray linoleum tile as I turn to face the testosterone-laden orchestra.

"Yes?" I ask.

"My office," he says as he takes three large steps to pass by me. I stand in place as each individual walks directly in front of me, none of them allowing me to move from where I am. After they're all beyond me, I see Sydney walking into the office with her bag slung over one shoulder and a rather large coffee in her hand.

"Syd, not a morning person today?" I say. She ignores this and maneuvers around the front desk. "Well?"

"Was here late yesterday. Figured it wouldn't hurt to only be on time for once." She looks down the hallway to where Zeile waits, arms folded, fatherly scorn riddled on his face.

"Military showed up and apparently I have to attend a meeting," I say. "Wanna join?"

"Don't you have to be invited?" she says as we drag ourselves toward the office.

"Come on, be the wingman at a bad wedding. You know you want to," I whisper.

"I'd rather not, considering the other case . . ."

"Great, come on." I pull her toward the room. "Might help Keets in the end."

I walk in and over to the right wall and lean against a low filing cabinet. Sydney props herself up beside me. The captain closes the door, fixes his jacket, and takes his seat behind his desk. It's then that I notice everyone is sitting but the two of us. It's funny in a way. I'm used to the common courtesy of a man offering his seat to a woman or someone in need. Considering Sydney's heels, it would have been a kind gesture.

Conversely, standing conveys an idea of domination or power. We are above all the men in the room. We can lean down or over them for intimidation or other oppressive maneuvers. It's a fascinating feeling knowing that these individuals switched everything up. It makes me apprehensive. Simply put, no one knowingly gives up that kind of leverage unless they want you to feel in control. The military is rather versed in this form of reverse psychology.

"Excuse me," I say to the man sitting closest to me. "Would you mind standing so my colleague could sit?"

He turns to the man with two stars on his shirt. At a slight nod from the older man, the younger gentleman immediately jumps to his feet. Sydney thanks him before sitting down. The silence in the room is palatable and rather irritating.

I break the tension. "Captain, is there a reason we're all in here? We do have open cases to handle."

"Yes, well, I'm sure Dr. Hayes informed you of our difficulty in identifying the victim." He leans back in his chair and pulls his tie down a bit as if getting oxygen is an issue. "Well, these gentlemen are here . . ."

The oldest-looking man, his white hair hidden under his hat, stands and leans on the captain's desk. He pulls his cap off with his right hand, places it under his left arm, and folds his hands together. The wrinkles of time wrap around his face like a labyrinth of memories.

"I'll get right to the point; everything brought up in this room is need to know only. The victim's name is Emelia Smith."

"Rank?" I ask.

"None. She's the daughter of a high-ranking official with access to sensitive information."

"And you think this is connected?" Sydney asks and pulls out a small notepad.

"Suffice it to say there is some concern this is premeditated."

"Can you give us anything more to work with here?" My tone is thick with irritation. Zeile notices and glares at me.

"Detective Steele, I can give you some documents, but I'm not at liberty to share anything further. We request you keep us informed of the case as it progresses." He waves his hands and the other men stand, salute, and exit the room. It's somewhat startling how synchronized their movements are. "We are well aware of the possible connection to your serial killer. That being said, we are capable of handling this case if necessary."

"I understand"—I glance at his badge—"Carter?"

"Major General Dennis Carter." He stands straighter, shoulders pushed back and his hands grasped behind his back.

"Major General, I appreciate you coming down here, but we can handle the case. If something comes up, we'll be in touch." Captain Zelle says from the safety behind his desk.

Carter walks right up to me. "Sergeant Everts was under my command for the majority of his career in the military. He's an excellent soldier and a better human being. You're lucky to have him as your partner," he says, holding his hand out in front of me.

He's missing most of his index finger and his thumbnail is badly scarred as if it was torn by a beast's teeth. My right hand fits in his. The small nub moves as if grabbing hold with a phantom finger. It's a haunting reminder of the ramifications of war. He can see my curiosity.

"Bullet," he says softly. "Blew it right off before I even knew what happened. Wrapped the stump in a bandanna and kept fighting." He releases my hand, fixes his hat back over his crew cut, and crisply turns and walks out.

"Now we have the military involved," Sydney says. "I guess this would be the 'exponentially bad' part."

"Depends on what hoops they make us jump through." The words fall out of my mouth as I try to wash the image of a bloody, handkerchief-covered stump out of my mind.

"If you find any evidence this is a copycat or made to look like the Carnation Killer, you are to hand it off immediately," Zeile says.

"Cap, we've never given up cases that quickly."

"Steele, pick and choose your battles. If it's outside of the parameters, pass it off. Understood?"

"Yes, sir," I say.

Zeile walks to the door and holds it open. Sydney leaves and heads to our office. I find myself lingering for a few moments to gather my thoughts.

"Steele?" Sydney calls from inside our office across the hall.

I expect the military dropped off boxes of information with various black lines riddling the pages. The office is going to be a clusterfuck of information. Taking a deep breath, I walk into the small, shared space to see our original case files still there. The boxes are lined up neatly, the board in its place, the floor clean. No mess. No extra information to sort through. Just Sydney standing in the middle, holding one solitary binder. It has to be at least three inches thick, but that's it.

"This is everything," she says. "And when I mean everything, I mean actual printouts of emails. Copies of things and whatever else. The best part . . ." She drops the binder on our desk and flips it open. Black covers the majority of every page. "It's like they don't really want help!"

I kick the door closed behind me, drop my stuff on my desk, and look over the binder. Scanning one email, I can see all names and important identifying information have been redacted. There are words here and there, clues that you can use to piece together an idea of the contents. It's not much and is a bit of a pain in the ass, but it's better than nothing.

"Devil's advocate," I say, flipping through some additional pages. "This is a national security issue and they gave us everything they could legally release."

"You really believe that?"

"I'm just too tired to fight the bullshit today. I want to focus and stop being five steps behind CK. I want to make sure this body can be tied to him, to make sure he's back and this isn't a superlative attempt at imitation." I stretch and my neck pops. I flop into my chair, and it squeals from age and usage. "You keep going through the notes from Olivia Anders. I'll see if anything pops out of these files.

This kind of tedious work requires noise-canceling headphones and my Broadway show tunes playlist. I used to have it play when I was writing in college. My ripped songs from *Phantom of the Opera*, *Les Misérables*, and *Grease* used to blast from my old lacking-in-bass computer speakers. Now that digital versions have replaced the old low-quality versions, the selection consists of some of those originals, but also movie musicals. Hugh Jackman's voice rings out quite often, telling me all kinds of positive things from *The Greatest Showman* to Lin Manuel Miranda rapping through *Hamilton*.

Flipping open the file, I see ninety percent of the first page is covered in redactions. Only the email, contact, and daughter's name are visible. There's no point in adding a page like this. It simply wastes my time and pads the binder. This might prove to be more difficult than I hoped. The second page holds more information regarding mailings and suspicious packages. No direct words connecting Emelia to these documents. Pulling out my tablet, I click it on and write some notes.

My eyes continue to skim across the lack of information when a hand suddenly appears directly in front of my face. My body jerks backward in surprise, promptly hitting the floor as the chair bounces off the wall behind me. While I was dead to the world, Logan came into the office and thought being two inches from my face was the appropriate course of action to gain my attention. If I had my weapon or mace, he'd be screaming in pain right now.

"Really, Logan?"

"What?" He holds his arms out as he snickers.

"Is there something you needed?" I say and pull myself back into my office chair.

"Our victim used Apple Pay for her bar tab the night before she was killed," he says. He holds out his tablet which shows the receipt. Seven dollars and fifty cents. "Probably only bought a beer and left."

"Or she paid before someone else covered the cost." I stand and grab my jacket. Sydney grabs the keys and waits by the door.

"Address?"

"I'll text it to you."

I usher Logan out of the office and Sydney locks it behind us. The three of us head down the hallway.

"You're doing the red carpet thing tonight, right?" he asks.

"Yes, I promised Hadley." I begin walking away from him, holding my phone in the air. "Still waiting for the address."

Sydney drives like my grandmother, her shoe off her right foot, driving with the tip of her big toe and sitting straight up. The GPS on her phone barks directions to Dreamers Den. The name sounds like a strip joint.

"So, red carpet event tonight?" Sydney asks.

"Yeah, Hadley has some festival premiere thing."

"It's really nice of you to support her."

"She's one of the Musketeers. Where she needs us, we follow, swords raised for battle." I'm staring out the window at the raindrops rolling sideways as we drive through the pothole-lined streets.

"Is it her new film or . . ."

"No. Something she did a long time ago. *Ties That Bind*, I think."

The cruiser turns right on Tenth Avenue and the hairs on my neck stand up. My attention stays on the street signs as we pass them. Forty-Five . . . Forty-Nine . . . Fifty-Five. Please keep going. Pass it. Go on.

Sydney turns left on Fifty-Seventh Street, settling my stomach before it erupts again when I see the bar sign. She stops the car and parks in front of a fire hydrant before putting the police placard in the windshield. I climb out, the rain pelting my head.

Walking into the bar brings me back to my twenties. There are wood barstools and high tables by the bar surrounded by televisions. The rest of the room has lower wood tables, benches, or chairs like any other place. The old lacquer chipping away is worse than when I last walked in. The stale smell of alcohol tickles the back of my throat, making me swallow the acidic bile.

"Steele?" Sydney asks.

"Yeah, good," I answer, forcing my heart to slow, my mind to disassociate. No one can hurt you here. It might be the same bar, but he's not here. Not anymore. Ownership has changed. It's different now. The words float through my mind, my fists clenched, my body feeling miles away from my pounding chest.

"Sorry, we're not open yet," a middle-aged man says. He walks toward us, drying his hands with a dishtowel.

"We're looking for the owner." Sydney holds her badge for the man to look over.

I don't move or show my badge. I use these moments to allow my panic attack to subside. The beating in my chest slows and my body feels like mine again.

"That would be me. Well, I'm one of them, anyway."

He extends his hand to Sydney. "Shawn Brandy."

She shakes his hand, her knuckles turning a lighter brown as she applies slightly higher than normal pressure. Handshakes are the most fascinating thing beyond signatures and reasons for murder. It's the first impression. A way to showcase your strength, professionalism, or weakness in the simplest of motions. I've had firm grips from all spectrums of society. A politician with a clammy but firm grip, nervous but still in control. A murderer with a firm, calm grip with a smile that reached his ears. He never showed an ounce of remorse and radiated pride in his crimes and diversity among his victims.

The worst handshake was that of a movie producer I met recently. Hadley introduced us proudly, and my hand was met with the oddest connection ever. His index and middle finger entered my palm, his thumb barely touching the outside of my hand. He shook weakly, almost feebly. There was no power, confidence, or comfort. My impression turned out to be true as Hadley filled us in with stories of his inability to make decisions. Apparently, he was better at writing checks than doing any actual work. He only desired to be known, loved, and lauded for work he was obviously unable to do on his own.

First impressions matter for this reason and more. It gives insight into who you are as a human being. Sydney bears down with her grip.

Right now, watching Mr. Brandy smiling, standing tall, and accepting the excess pressure from a short, Black woman with a badge is impressive. He's not intimidated. He simply pulls his hand back, shakes it out, and smiles at her.

"I guess what they say is very true." He smiles.

"That would be?"

"Short but powerful packages." He waves to the barstools. "Something like that anyway. So, what can I do for you both?"

"Have you seen this woman? She might have been here Tuesday evening." I hold up my cell phone with Emelia Smith's image on it.

"Yeah, she's a regular. I think she's a graduate student. Good kid." He leans against the bar. "Something happen to her?"

"Do you have camera footage? Receipts?" I ask, ignoring his question.

He drops the rag on the bar top and crosses his arms. "We have footage, but it's aimed at our employees. Ensures our pours are accurate and money isn't being skimmed. Beyond that, I don't have much. Everything is digital and eco-friendly. Receipts are emailed."

"Was she with anyone that night?" Sydney interjects.

"I really don't know. My partner was helping out with the bar area. I made sure security, the food, and music were all going strong."

"Is your partner here?" I ask.

"No, Karl teaches English to the undergrads next door. Grammar Nazi by day and bar owner at night."

"Karl?" I ask.

"Schlect. Karl Schlect, my business partner."

"Would you know if he's there now?" Sydney follows up.

"At school? No, no classes on Friday. He's taking care of my mom tonight, but he'll be here tomorrow around ten in the morning to start the day."

I move away from the bar and shiver one last time as my eyes dart around the place. Pictures of various high school and college teams litter the walls. Some autographed memorabilia of older sports stars hang in frames or shadow boxes. Everything about this place screams college and sports bar. A framed image of two teenage boys kneeling on their helmets sits above the bar behind Brandy's head. Thankfully the design is very different from when I was here last. "Why did you change the name?" I ask without thinking.

"We hated it. Dive Bar was generic, and Karl wanted something that supported the local college and community. We've got so many people with hopes and dreams of the future. He wanted Dreamer's Den. I preferred something less porn sounding, but he had more money so he named it."

"Odd name for a college sports bar," Sydney pipes up.

"Yeah well, I wanted University Hall to give kids a proper sounding place of entry. Could you imagine telling your parents you went to University Hall to study? It would be an easy cover. But sadly, those who cut the checks, have all the power."

"Would have been a better choice." My monotone voice hits the surrounding walls. My eyes focus on the small booth in the back-left corner. I can still hear his laugh as he hit on a young woman barely of legal age for intercourse, let alone anywhere near drinking age. I can still smell the stale cigars on his shirt, feel his calloused hands on my young skin and the subsequent pain that followed.

"Hey, you okay?" Sydney asks as her hand on my shoulder jolts me out of my memories.

"Yeah, I think we're done for now." I pull out my card and hand it to Shawn. "If you can think of anything else, please let us know."

Walking out the door, the setting sun hits the tall buildings, casting shadows along the streets. The mix of light and dark grays mimic the swirling emotions running rampant through my chest. The secrets of my youth come up my esophagus in the form of bile as the memory of cigar smoke remains in my nasal cavity. My brain tricks my body into feeling as though the pain, fear, and insecurity is fresh and new. The trunk I've hidden my darkest demons in has begun to crack. I know the nightmares of my teenage and early college years will revisit me again. The weight of my innocence lost all those years ago will prevent me from closing my eyes.

I'm being assaulted all over again.

Chapter Five

As we pull up to the premiere, rolling spotlights and people packed behind police barricades fill both sides of the street. Media and camera flashes light up an already bright area. The scrolling jumbotron background with *NY Indy Fest* and various advertisers repeats for what looks like the full avenue.

"We'll be pulling up shortly, ma'am," the driver says. His bleached white gloves stop at the base of his thumb. A faded, blueish-green symbol tattoo shows against his pale skin before the cuff of his white shirt and the layer of his black suit. His short haircut holds his hat in place. Through the windshield, the backlog of limos comes into view—a half dozen in line, like planes on a runway.

"Someone from the production team will come to get us. There'll be people on the carpet telling us how to progress down the carpet, okay?" Hadley says as she shifts her breasts in her strapless top. "Why did I decide to wear this? I'm falling out of this thing."

"You're fine, Had. Just breathe," Frankie says. Her long hair is up in loose curls, bouncing with every turn of her head. The floor-length red dress with the slit up the left leg, along with her five-inch heels, shows off her stunning frame. The desire to take her home for myself is beaten back by my desire to let the world see the beauty that Frankie and Hadley embody inside and out. Let the world see how lucky Logan and I are.

"You okay there, Steele?" Logan asks, sitting across from me. His tuxedo is perfectly fitted to his surprisingly fit frame.

"Yeah, just thinking," I answer.

"Leave work at the precinct," Frankie's voice whispers in my ear. "For one night, just enjoy this."

My fingers clasp hers like they've done so many times before. Memories from earlier in the day creep back in—the smells, sounds, and feelings, as if my worst memories were currently happening. My hand tightens around hers, and I know she's concerned and worried. The overwhelming feeling of fear, the unknown, and people staring at me cause an anxiety attack to push against my inner wall of strength. It takes Frankie's grip and her previous words to help me keep it at bay. My mother singing a lullaby to me in German rings through my mind, and slowly I feel more like myself again.

The door opens, revealing a long, red-carpet-covered sidewalk. Never releasing Frankie's hand, I step out of the limo with the driver's assistance. My boot heel touches the ground, but the sound is muffled by the cacophony of camera shutters. My tailored tuxedo is comfortable except for the lack of a shirt under the low-cut coat. Hadley insisted I wear something more modern. I initially pushed back until I saw how my fiancée looked at me. I'd wear a potato sack if it gave me the same desired expression.

The two of us stand hand in hand slightly off to the side. A woman in front of me with a headset and a clipboard barks some directions into the small boom mic by her mouth. Hadley exits the limo, and the noise increases tenfold. Her sleek, black gown hits the floor as the driver ensures it misses the puddle by the curb. Logan holds out his elbow for her to take, which she does. The woman with the headset waves them down the carpet immediately.

"Once they hit the second mark on the carpet, you two will go down, okay?" she screams over the throng of fans. "Okay, go!" she says quickly. Her clipboard presses into my back and pushes me forward.

I take a few tentative steps down the walkway, and bright lights instantly blind the two of us. Frankie pulls me closer, her arm twisting around mine. Ahead of us are reporters' voices, fans, and photographers screaming for Hadley to turn toward them. We hit the first piece of tape and turn to face the wall of media. The flashes coat us like a torrential downpour. My eyes dart around, looking for a focal point. Once I find one, it dies only to pop up somewhere else. Like a cat teased with a laser pointer, we look around and shift our weight as the woman nearby tells us to walk to the second spot. Rinse and repeat. At the end of the tsunami of discomfort, a reporter waits to cause more anxiety for me.

"Hi, how are you?" she asks casually.

"We're doing lovely. How are you?" Frankie answers and drags me by the hand forward into the lobby. Dealing with the press is the last thing either of us wants.

"I didn't know if she was done," I say.

"I know, but I was. I know you were. Honey, we're not built for this. We can smile and look pretty, but I don't give a fuck who you're wearing. Your jewelry is your grandmother's, your nails are chipped, and don't think I didn't notice your side piece on your ankle. This is not our scene." She spins, grabs the lapel of my tuxedo jacket, and pulls me close.

"Be careful; I'm not wearing a bra."

Her eyes slink down my bare skin as her face begins to flush. "Then let's go enjoy this evening before I rip the rest of this tux off right here." She kisses me passionately before pulling me down to the end of the mass of people and into the building.

✱✱✱

The fancy awards dinner was nice, but food that was edible would have been appreciated. I poke my filet mignon with my fork and the surface bends but barely gives. There's a green concoction on my plate which is a mix of spinach, Brussels sprouts, and what I think is bok choy. I eat the bread on the table; it's simple, with no crazy spices or ingredients I can't spell. These awards dinners always have great desserts though. Best to save room for that.

I look over at Logan, who's having as much luck with his steak as I had with mine. Our eyes meet. He stabs his steak once more and gives up.

"I was thinking about the case," Logan says before going off on a tangent. "How in the hell do you overcook a filet like this? This is brutal—"

"Logan!" I cut him off. "You were thinking about the case?"

"Oh. Yeah. Well, this guy has to be really smart, you know? None of the women he's killed really used social media or had a significant digital footprint of their meeting. Like nothing posted of the guy at all. That's like stupidly difficult right now considering how people literally *live* for likes, hearts, or retweets," Logan says. He's had a few glasses of wine and is slightly slurring his words.

"Maybe," I say. "But it could also be that the killer and victim were too busy with one another to bother posting images or tweets. I've never understood the desire to post your entire life or a fucking sex selfie. It's a bit personal, plus those images are forever. So, to me, that's not really out of the ordinary."

Logan's cheeks are red. Significantly red.

"Logan?" Frankie prods a bit after hearing the last bit. "Do you and Hadley . . ."

Logan changes gears quickly. "I've got my team working on the cell phones of all the victims. Just in case they took photos but didn't post them and he deleted them. Maybe the phone pings a coordinate somewhere; it could help."

"Okay, let me know if they follow some kind of pattern that you can make sense of."

An older woman approaches a podium and begins to speak. "Hello everyone, thank you so much for coming this evening." She looks around the room, her elegant, black, sequined dress catching the lights from above. She moves her foot slightly out of her overly high heels. She barely moves her mouth and shows no real facial expression, possibly due to the thick spray-paint makeup. Her words continue to be blurred out by the scratching of her manicured nails against the wood—nails that could scoop your eye out in one motion. "And tonight, we honor Hadley Moreno for her contributions to the independent film community, her boundless talent that takes us to new heights, and her tireless effort supporting cancer research projects."

Hadley stands there, elegant, stunning, beaming with pride as the audience claps furiously. The photographers continue to click away, but in my mind, I see flashbacks of her struggle. All those tears from failed auditions, the fear of the next one, the terror of actually landing the role she wanted, to now. Her confidence, the talent shining through the screens to hit the eyes of those who once overlooked her. There's a pride boiling in our chests seeing her success. I wish Victor could be here, but he and Lillian had to work the case.

The applause slows, and one by one the crowd all sit back down. Hadley holds a piece of paper in her hand, probably a speech written from one of her agents or the new publicist. Words that might mean something to them, but likely don't fully express her thoughts. After a few seconds of silence, she folds the paper back up and places it to the side.

"My publicist gave me a beautiful speech to read, but I don't want to bore you with name dropping. Thank you to everyone who has ever given me guidance, all of my teachers, managers, and agents through the years. You know who you are." She pauses and blinks furiously. "This is my first major recognition for anything I've done, and it's going to mess up my face!"

She and the audience chuckle slightly. "I've dreamed of standing in front of my peers holding an award since I was old enough to hold a brush and look in the mirror. I would recite the lines of a film, pretending to be the lead heroine saving the day. I would reenact every memorable scene, perfecting my accents along the way. My mother, bless her soul, never truly understood my desire to play someone other than myself. She demanded I get a backup degree, and I did. If she only knew that pushing me toward my degree would surround me with people who supported my true desire." She pauses, takes a deep breath, and looks over to our table.

Frankie reaches back and takes hold of my hand. Her grip is firm, comforting. She knows I dislike attention, especially when it comes to compliments or gratitude.

"I met Jasmine Steele when we were both blinded by the lights of the fictitious worlds of our own making. Studying the mind, seeing how we could bend words or actions to our will. As I'm sure many of you have read, she's a workaholic with a tiny human to take care of. Yet, she always makes time for her friends . . . her family. I might get a text at three in the morning asking about my audition the previous day, but she always reached out. It's why I leaned on her for support when *Ties That Bind* came across my desk. You know someone loves you when they show you the proper way to handcuff another human being," she says suggestively. "I can never thank you enough for that by the way."

Logan drops his face into his hands while the room erupts in laughter. "Truthfully, this award is because of the village I have around me. My best friends, my protectors, and my chosen family. I can't imagine being on this ride without you all. Thank you for the yesterdays and for all the tomorrows. I love you all." She turns back to the audience. "Thank you."

She slowly descends the stage, but several people stop her along the way. Logan, looking red in the face from embarrassment, but also from tears, continues clapping. The pride he has in his girlfriend shines through. I was unsure of their relationship at first, but seeing them like this is a blessing.

My phone vibrates in my pocket with a new message.

"You okay?" Frankie asks.

I read the message. "I have to go. Victor says it's important, left a file on my desk. Tell Hadley I'm proud of her."

Frankie kisses me quickly. "Don't stay out too late, okay?"

I smile and kiss her one more time before heading toward the door.

***

I hear yelling as I walk out of the elevator. It seems to be coming from my office. "What the . . .?"

Walking through the desks in that direction and hearing the wolf whistles from other officers on the night shift just irritates me more. Say I look nice; don't whistle or ogle me like I'm a pound of bacon freshly out of the oven.

One step into my office, and it sounds like a warzone. Sydney stands as tall as possible, her hands firmly grasping her hips.

"If you'd stop yelling for five minutes, I would explain," she says.

"What? That a soldier's daughter was killed? That I've been put on the sidelines because of a minor injury and you've made yourself comfortable in my chair?" Will's voice rises higher. His right arm waves around to emphasize each word. This is not like my partner at all.

"Hey," I say, trying to stop this confrontation.

"The captain said you were on desk duty and not to bother you. You're a liability out in the field until you're cleared!" Sydney ignores my interruption.

"I've had blood pouring in my eyes and still managed to complete my mission. I'm not a liability to anyone," Will shouts.

"Well, you're not in the desert anymore!"

"That's good, because you wouldn't survive one minute!"

"Shut up!" My voice booms over their heads, bouncing off the walls and echoing into the main entrance area.

The two of them finally turn around to see me standing there, dressed to the nines, angry and frustrated. I stare at Will before pointing to my chair. He slowly moves, his body showing signs of discomfort with every motion. Once he manages to get into my chair, I look over to Sydney and point to her desk. Shaking her head, she follows suit.

"I was out at an important event, and I get a text message from Victor telling me the precinct turned into Thunderdome. I show up and you two are at each other's throats in my fucking office."

"I'm sorry he did that—"

"Stop, I'm talking. Not you, Will." I turn quickly to Sydney and raise my hand to stop her from even thinking about responding. "So, Will is going to speak first. Then Sydney. If you talk over one another, turn this into a screaming match or a whose dick is bigger, I swear on my mother's grave I will go ahead and kick you out of this office. Then I'll go to the captain and have a write-up put in each of your jackets. I don't give a fuck. I'm tired, my feet fucking hurt, and I could be eating some five-star chocolate right now!" I look back and forth between them like I'm at a tennis match. "Good?" They nod. "Will, go."

"A friend of mine called me about the Carnation Killer's latest victim. I came here to talk to Captain Zeile about being reinstated so I can help. I came in and Detective Locke was not only sitting at my desk but also threatening me."

"I—"

"Think before you open your mouth right now. So not in the mood for sandbox bullshit," I say, shooting daggers at Sydney. She slinks back in her chair as if admonished by her mother. "How did she threaten you?"

"She was going to turn me into the captain."

"You said you had planned on speaking to him. That doesn't make sense."

"He refused to fully reinstate me," Will says softly.

"So, you're on desk duty." He nods. "Let me get this straight. You spoke to the boss, he said no, and you walked into our office to investigate anyway?"

"Her father was one of us."

"Yes, he was, but that doesn't give you permission to come in here and stir the pot." I turn to Sydney. "You, speak."

"I was looking over some evidence Victor sent up when Detective Everts stormed in demanding to see Emelia Smith's file. I refused, and he started sorting through everything looking for it. It got a bit heated."

"A bit? More like a Bette Davis and Joan Crawford fight!" The two of them look at me, confusion evident on their faces. "Jesus, look it up, people. Fucking classic Hollywood feud! Whatever. Look, here's what's going to happen. Will, Sydney is going to use your desk until such a time that you are fully cleared to return. And you are going to do whatever the boss wants you to do so that I can get my partner back. If we have any questions about the current case, we will ask you. If there is something you can assist us with that won't endanger your well-being, we will ask. Sydney will not piss you off, step on toes, or otherwise irritate the fuck out of you by being too close to the book. Am I clear?"

They both nod. It hits me that Will was supposed to be babysitting Chase during this altercation.

"Who's watching Chase?"

"Maya and the girls. *Star Wars* marathon. He refused to leave because the good ones were going to start."

"If I may?" Sydney asks, standing with a file folder in her hands. "I know you're on desk duty, but maybe there is something you can investigate for me. It will require getting a lot of information over the phone and dealing with red tape and other items. I know Dr. Ryan is also looking over the psychological profiles."

"What is it?" Will asks, hopeful.

Sydney walks across the room and hands him a file. I'm sure it's the Keets case. She's always wanted his input and pull with other people. Watching the two of them start to talk like human beings, I grab Victor's file off my desk, walk out of the door, and run into the captain.

"My office. Now."

"Sir, I know what this looks like, but I'm sure—"

"Close the door behind you, detective."

I do as I'm told before sitting in front of the captain's chair. His expression reminds me of my mother's "I'm not angry with you, just beyond disappointed" look. God, I hated that more than a spanking.

"I promise you Will and Sydney are working through it. That . . . outburst won't happen again."

"I don't care about Locke and Everts. They don't want to work together, I'll transfer them both or take their damn badges. I want to know who the hell you've been talking to. We agreed, no press!" He drops a copy of the early edition of tomorrows *New York Post* right in front of me.

My face, with Sydney right behind me, plastered on the cover. Various sensational words riddle the headline, but there are no images of the new victim. Flipping over to the article, the headline grabs me: **STEELE vs CARNATION KILLER.** Holy shit. They make it sound like a tournament bracket. Scanning over the first few rows of information, it's obvious someone has been making stuff up.

"Captain, you know this isn't true, right? They're using public information to formulate these ideas. I never spoke to anyone or issued any ultimatum to the killer. They say it's a person of color, mid to late fifties from various witness accounts! We have no witnesses to speak of at all. This is utter bullshit."

"If you're lying to me, Steele, this means your badge. You understand?"

"Yes, sir."

"Then I'll handle it. Get out of my office." He grabs the phone, most likely calling our public relations department. This is going to require a statement from the department, hopefully without my assistance. The door clicks shut behind me as the captain's voice reaches my ears.

"We've got a situation." That's an understatement.

Pulling out my phone, I send Victor a quick text asking about this new evidence. Within seconds, the reply comes through. He's no longer in the office but can meet me there in the morning to discuss it . . . on a Saturday. His next text is short, all caps, and to the point: READ THE FILE.

I'm not looking forward to it.

Chapter Six

The autopsy freezers line the wall in a meaningless grid, bodies stacked on top of one another, void of life by design and reality. Just that sterling silver look with a matching handle, a business-card-sized opening for a typed-up name. It's clinical, efficient, and still sends chills down my spine. It's a place no normal person should ever see.

The last images of my loved ones being housed inside remain forever etched in my brain. The pasty-white look of my mother's face and skin. My frail-looking father, who died without telling me he loved me. My sister-in-law, her face deformed from glass, metal, and parts of a tree from the car wreck that took her life. My brother, his legs torn and tattered from the dashboard. The lack of healing and harsh stitches—the remnants of life-saving procedures . . . pictures that linger behind to torment. It replaces the beautiful memories and flashes in front of your eyes when you think of them. It's why Victor never moves the sheet below the neck.

"You're early," Victor says, opening the door to his closet-sized office and dropping his bag on the desk.

"Couldn't sleep," I say. I can't help staring at the squares of death.

"Dreams of the past or something more sinister?"

"Aren't they one and the same?"

He slides into his white coat as he glides across the plain linoleum flooring. I can feel his eyes on me, trying to figure out the meaning behind my words.

"You told Sydney you found something new?" I say to change the discussion.

"Yes, but I'm not sure how much I can help with it. Lillian has to run her tests."

"Vic, pretend we're in kindergarten; more show and tell, less waving around of arms," I say.

"Right." He walks over to the second column of compartments. "I'm surprised the military hasn't removed her body from us yet."

"Conspiracy theories just grow like vines in your mind, don't they?" I say.

"No need to get snippy." He pulls on the latch and pushes the door open. "Just wondering if those binders show anything or was it all just a Sharpie investment."

"It would be printer ink, not a Sharpie. I won't ask why you were looking at evidence in my locked office."

"Detective Locke was there, and I only glanced at the one binder. She was reading the other one. Rather flustered with it, I might add." He pulls out the long tray and folds back the white sheet.

Emelia Smith lies there, cold and rigid, her perpetually tan-colored skin now almost an alabaster white except for the purple and black outlines of fingers. The bruising covering both sides of her neck showcases the ferocity of her end.

"What did you find?"

"Basic signs of sexual intercourse. Like the others, her vaginal cavity was filled with a water and bleach combination. The body was washed down with the same solution, so any possible DNA evidence on the skin was too contaminated to even attempt to run."

"Then how can you be sure they had sex before death?"

"Bruising around her entryway. Based on that, I would conclude she and her killer had vigorous relations during her death."

"You make it sound so technical." I move away from the body, "If that's all you found, it's not very helpful. Everything you've mentioned is what we have on all of the other women."

"True. Emelia gave us something else." Victor covers her body back up and slides the metal tray holding the body back into the locker until it clicks. He closes the door, putting her back into darkness.

"You should have led with that," I say.

Victor ignores my snarkiness and walks around to a new mobile computer center. "I needed to show you the basics first. You know damned well if I showed you the new stuff, you would rush out to Lillian's office and harass her without having the full picture."

I say nothing as he begins to pound away at the defenseless keyboard. An X-ray pops up on the screen, and he turns the monitor to face me. The dental images of Emelia cover the screen. A small set of circles covers her upper and lower teeth.

"What am I looking at?"

"Emelia's dental X-ray. Those circles are where we found skin cells."

"She bit him," I say, my voice lower but tinged with some hope.

"I sent the samples over to Lillian. Maybe we'll get lucky and get a hit."

"Possible, but we wouldn't be able to connect it to the other cases. Besides, it would show he was there, but we couldn't possibly get the jury to believe that teeth make the killer." I turn my attention back to the grid of metal doors.

"Worked on Ted Bundy."

"Yes, who had a reputation and accusations in several over states at the time of his arrest in Florida."

"Yes, well . . . maybe this individual has a history we don't know about." He continues trying to defend his moot point.

"Why didn't he clean her up? Brush her teeth? He must have known she bit him hard enough. It doesn't fit the profile."

"None of the other victims had clean teeth. Residue from drinks, previous meals, all matching their stomach contents. Maybe he just didn't see the need."

"What do you always say?"

"Behavior and science are black-and-white. You can try to cover it up, deviate, or straight-up lie, but the essence of truth always remains."

"Exactly. The essence of truth. Either something changed or it was a deliberate action. Maybe Frankie can figure it out." I turn, hit the elevator button, and wait for the door to swish open.

"There's one other option."

"What's that?" I ask, looking over my shoulder.

"Copycat? Maybe it was a hit and they made a mistake?"

"Bare hands or gloves?"

"Bare hands."

"I'll have Lillian compare all of them. If everything lines up, we'll know for sure." I step into the elevator and head down to the science lab.

None of this makes any sense. The military getting involved just wasted my time. It might not be a lot, but it deviated our attention, and that's never smart. It took a day or so to almost definitively prove that they have no connection to this case. I don't believe in coincidences. There's something more to this than they're allowing us to see.

The crime lab is busy as usual. People roll on their stools from desks to their microscopes. Reminds me of the fun my brother and I had at my grandparents' business. We would race each other down the hallway in office chairs. The dents in the wall showed our passion and competitiveness. The fact that they were never fixed just proved that my family cared more about our memories and fun than they did proper behavior. At least when there was no one else around. A family-run business and the employees become the family of choice. It's all gone now.

Lillian walks up and stands next to me. "Jasmine?"

"Lillian."

"One of these days I'm going to remove the wheels from those damn things."

I'm watching a young woman bouncing on her stool to the beat of the music in her headphones. "To prevent contamination or mishandling of evidence?"

"Well, there's that, but also because half of them are uncoordinated and end up falling. It's a horrid amount of paperwork. Besides, I've always had to stand, and misery loves company."

"You're evil. You know that?"

Lillian smiles and turns toward her office, waving me along as she struts. Her designer heels make a clickety-clack sound as they meet the white linoleum flooring. A male intern passes her and stumbles over his feet. Lillian has that aura about her—the sex appeal mixed with a massive amount of intimidation. She makes no apologies for her ability, looks, or intelligence. She has yet to be put off by anything other than Victor, of course. He's the only one who can easily knock her off-kilter.

"I'm assuming Victor sent you my way." It's a statement, not a question.

"Something about new evidence he sent to your department." As I follow her, my Timberland boots squeak and echo down the hall, bringing unwanted attention my way.

Lillian walks up to a wall panel and places her hand on a screen. After a few seconds, it turns green. She then leans forward for a retinal scan. All this security around the lab, and I can see Logan hacking it in minutes. Nothing is ever truly protected from the will of those with stubborn streaks, funding, or governmental threats.

The glass doors retract with a swishing sound that reminds me of the entryways in *Star Trek*. They part and slide to opposite sides as we walk into the middle of the room. I've never been in Lillian's personal lab before. One wall is entirely comprised of floor-to-ceiling shelves. There are glass beakers of various sizes along the middle row down the whole wall that beckon me to pick one up. I shove my hands into my pockets with force.

The doors shut behind me, making the same sound as when they opened. Lillian walks into the room and grabs her long, white lab coat. She slips her arms through the sleeves with ease, and flips her hair over the collar.

I take in the rest of the room. The other two walls are lined with a countertop, stools, and file drawers every few feet. On top are several microscopes and various high-end machines that I'm sure do things beyond my comprehension. In the center of the room is an island housing several computer monitors, keyboards, and a printer on each end. Boxes labeled *Carnation Killer* are stacked on the floor against the island.

"You okay, detective?" Lillian asks. It's then I realized I haven't moved from the doorway.

"It's just . . . I've never been in here before."

"Want the dime tour then?" she asks, and I nod. "Okay, the room is bulletproof glass. Everything in here is tempered so if it does break, it won't shatter. The machines on the left wall all deal with liquid evidence, and the ones on the right wall deal with everything else. Everything is hands off. Got it?"

"Yup." I walk right in front of the row of computer monitors, hands firmly in my pockets.

"Wonderful." Lillian begins to click a mouse and frantically types away at her keyboard. She doesn't look up but asks, "What's with the hands in the pockets?"

"Bull in a china shop," I say, shrugging my shoulders.

"You're not a child, so please remove them. Rest assured everything is insured to the nines should you not heed my previous warnings." She continues to type.

"Still, my mother would kick my ass if I touched anything. It's drilled into my genetic coding."

"Understood." The printer roars to life, the gears rotating, the paper sliding from the tray with laser ink emblazoned on it. A hot page shoots into the tray as the printer sighs to a stop. "So, we know the other victims' bodies were void of any testable DNA."

"They were degraded with bleach or contaminated in some other way."

"Precisely." She grabs the page and looks it over. "Emelia had testable quantities in her mouth." She hands me the page. "No hits in the system, but if you get a suspect, we can compare samples."

Grabbing the sheet, I look over the peaks and valleys of the reds, blues, greens, and blacks. Everything that uniquely makes us who we are plotted out in simple charts. No one else will ever match this charting. Your mother and father each match about half of it, but this is my killer. On a piece of paper, my serial killer now has a profile. It's a chilling moment. This is the first tactile thing I have on him.

"It doesn't make sense to me. He consistently goes to the trouble of concealing his identity, but then he makes a gaffe like this? He must have felt himself being bitten. Why not clean her mouth?" I'm still staring at the profile.

"That's Dr. Ryan's expertise. Maybe she or one of her colleagues can shed some light on it. Not my area. I'm only the one who can connect Mr. Smith here to the other murders."

"Everything we have on the others is circumstantial at best. Bruising patterns, MO. I'm running on empty, doc," I say.

"Plant genetics."

"Excuse me?"

Lillian moves to another workstation and begins to type on a different keyboard, and a television set resting near the doors comes to life. An image of a molecular slide appears on the screen. "Plant DNA. The DNA is as unique as ours. I can't match them to each other like we do with humans due to the chloroplasts, but I can tell you the fertilizer ratio used."

"I don't see how this helps or what it means, truthfully."

"The fertilizer. Used to grow the carnations." By my blank look, she can tell I'm rolling blank tape. She continues. "Before I transferred here, I worked a case involving a body burned in a barrel. No physical evidence was available due to the intense heat. The coroner identified the body with dental records, but forensically we had very little to work with."

Lillian types away and the television screen switches to a gallery of crime scene photos: a myriad of trees, a small clearing, an old, rusted barrel, but nothing discernable that draws my attention.

"Middle of the woods. How'd the barrel and body get there. Tire tracks?" I ask.

"Some generic ones that are on every Ford F150 in the area. Too many candidates, but it was used to support the case against the perpetrator."

"Sounds violent, personally. Bad relationship? Family drama?"

"Thinking like a true detective and less like a scientist." She chuckles a bit. "Lived with her father, no significant other. Only child. Father had an alibi but it couldn't be corroborated."

"Friends? Coworkers? Online presence?"

"All different accounts and statements." She clicks on some photos to enlarge them. The angle shows a blue barrel with several rust spots under the tree. The victim's boney arm sticks up from the center.

"Perception and personal experience tend to filter what we perceive or think," I say. "You see something a specific way and express what you hear or read in a way that your brain comprehends. That's why I don't rely solely on eyewitness testimony."

"Precisely. Science, however, never lies. We found a partial number on the barrel. That led us to the main company who made them. Then we found trace elements inside the container that led us to a manure factory."

"How many employees are using that model truck?"

"Fifteen." She hits the keyboard again and opens several images of test results and a newspaper article. "I keep a protected folder with this information inside. To inspire me, motivate me. When I feel like I've hit a brick wall, it reminds me that anything can be deciphered with determination, creativity, and ingenuity."

"What did you do?"

"We were given permission to cut the tree down. Before you get upset, once the case was over, we planted several more as per our agreement with the town." She highlights a photo showing the cross section of the tree. "We took several samples for DNA extraction, chemical testing, and several slices of the tree to examine its rings. I won't go into the details of the science behind it, but we found there were trace chemicals in the samples that shouldn't be there. We also found a disruption in the rings where a chemical was introduced from an outside source. When we figured it out, we got the composition of the accelerant and compared it to the owners of those trucks. Her father's truck used that specific brand of gas from a gas station around the block from his house. The tires matched, and he was responsible for unloading the barrels at his firm. It was enough to convict."

"But not a slam dunk. How can this help us with flowers?"

"The nitrogen, phosphorus, and potassium levels could be tested, and it seems the fertilizer used was a five-ten-five system. Pretty common. After further testing, I found trace elements of micronutrients from seaweed extracts, borax, and other complex sugars. I searched the databases for fertilizers matching this breakdown, and I came back with Age-Old Bloom. It's an organic one sold online. And in a few stores locally."

"It's not perfect, but it's a start. How many stores is 'a few'?"

"About fifty."

"Can you email the list to Logan and tell him to cross-reference all the information we have with the store locations? Maybe he can narrow it down." I stare at the label of organic liquid feed.

"I compared all the carnations; they all were grown with the same compounds. So, I can say this person is probably growing these on their own. You find the source, I can compare them."

"Unless you add bleach."

"Sugar and a penny. Helps with the pH levels. My mother had a green thumb. I can't keep a cactus alive."

"Thanks, Lillian." I walk out of her office and down the hall.

Whenever we had flowers in my house, my mother always added a small amount of Clorox bleach to the water mixture. Her carnations would last longer than average and always seemed to be so vibrant. My grandmother did the same. It was something she learned as a child growing up on a farm and had passed it down. The idea rolls around my mind like a pinball.

I need Frankie's brain . . . now.

Frankie's receptionist sits behind her desk, headset firmly covering one ear and a boom mic hovering near her mouth. Her long, manicured nails graze the surface of her cell phone as I stand leaning on the wood, waiting for her to notice me. The office phone drags her attention away from the iPhone as she answers. The slight shrill of her voice reminds me of an older woman working as a phone operator in the 1950s.

Her attention glides up to me and she raises her index finger before turning away again. The bright yellow nail polish makes me more aware of the sharpness of those weapons. The creative side of my brain wanders with thoughts of a villain who gouges eyes out with a sharp middle fingernail.

The sign hanging above the desk never fails to bring me back to reality. A smirk forms on my face, natural and impossible to stop. Frankie's last name in full three-dimensional block letters with her two other partners' names. She got her degree and worked her way up from a small assistant sitting in on cases, studying and writing up all the reports, transcribing notes, and all that other shit work no one likes.

"Jasmine?" Frankie's melodic voice calls from behind me.

"Out of the office meeting?" I ask.

"I met my brothers for coffee since I had a bit of an open schedule right now." She motions to the hallway to her office.

"How are they?" I toss out nervously.

"Enjoying the city. It's been a while since they've been here. Waylon still hopes he'll run into someone famous. Wade made sure they hit that soup place from *Seinfeld*." She opens the door to her office. "I never understood the popularity of that show. Made no sense to me." I walk into the office but don't sit down. She closes the door and places her jacket on the coat rack by the door. "It's not like you to show up unannounced, and I doubt you want to hear about your future brothers-in-law."

"Bleach!" The words tumble out of my mouth as I begin to pace the office.

"Okay, a simple text to pick some up would have been sufficient."

"The killer. Bleach. He's covering up his tracks; that part's pretty obvious. I mean, whenever you have soiled whites or something that needs to be disinfected, you use bleach. It manages to eradicate everything if you use it correctly. Theoretically, it gives you a clean slate. It allows you to use the shirt again, to try and not get Mom's tomato sauce on it," I rattle off with my arms moving in the air. The Italian in me is overwhelming the German politeness as my boots continue to squeak, slide, and whine across the hardwood floors.

"Jasmine . . ."

"The question is why? Is the flower more about purity than the historical secret admirer reference point?"

"Jasmine . . ."

"He grows them, nurtures them to maturity, shows them care and love. Then he rips them from their roots, and they're destined to die in a few weeks." Frankie stands in front of me, blocking my path. My legs move of their own volition, turning me around, and I continue. "How can someone so meticulous with his tools, calling cards, and his routine slip up like this? Did he want us to find out? Did he know? If he made a mistake, what does it actually mean?"

"Jasmine!" Frankie's hands grab my biceps, stopping my forward motion. She holds my gaze for a few seconds until my breathing slows back to a normal pace. "Would you mind slowing down and explaining to me what the hell you're rambling on about?"

"Carnation Killer."

"What about him?"

Her hands fall from my arms and part of me misses the instant connection. I walk over to the couch and fall into its plush, comforting embrace.

"The flowers are homegrown. He uses a specific fertilizer that is sold mainly online, but also in a few stores locally."

"He wouldn't shop online. Not for something like this."

"I agree. Everything we've got says it would go outside of his profile," I say.

"Yes, and online orders can be traced. PayPal, credit cards, whatever—they all have a digital signature. He'd consider it more dangerous since you provide account numbers. Then the police would be able to see what else the person has purchased, where they've shopped, etcetera," she says, leaning back on her desk. The palms of her hands rest on the top of the wood as her fingers curl underneath, tapping in time to her words.

"Well, yes. That's very 'detective-y' of you."

"I am marrying one, you know. Now, what does bleach have to do with this? Beyond your ramblings, which I have no reference point for."

I slowly begin speaking. "Mom and Grandma always put bleach in their flowers. They said it would help them live longer. I think he's using it as an image representing their souls being kept alive and a clean slate for the afterlife."

Frankie stands up and runs her hands through her hair before folding them in front of her. "Wow," she says, looking at me seriously. "That is a lot to unpack and process. Do you have any psychological inference that led you down this path?"

"Just my instinctual bullshit from the degree and years of being a cop."

"Right. Well, that's wonderful, but it won't hold up in court." She loosens her arms and drops one hand to her right hip. "I haven't started an official profile yet, but your theory is plausible. It might fit."

"In our profiling class, we learned to look for the little things. The one aspect of your personality that seeps through regardless of your best attempts to hide it."

"While that may be true, we learned that in our handwriting analysis class." She smiles at me. "Our profiling professor taught via the monotonous textbook, and we were both irritated the entire semester."

"I can't believe the professor retired."

"Died. She died before the start of the fall term."

"Shit, didn't know that. Regardless, my point is, I think this guy grows the flowers to what he considers perfection. They're devoid of color, dyes, and any nonorganic chemicals. When they're ready, he finds the perfect victim to accept his offering. They meet and begin to have consensual sex before he kills them during his climax. Then he cleans the bodies of any trace of the act. They get a clean slate for the ferryman," I say.

"Psychopathic tendencies abound. You might be on the right track, but we also know flowers have a short lifespan. If he waits for the flowers to bloom, then picks his victims, they might not last that long."

"Not every flower has a mate," I answer. "Some are destined to roam the earth until they die, alone and unwanted. Like him."

"Did you have one too many energy drinks? You're being really philo-sophical without any prompting. Or alcohol," she says.

"No. Just thinking too much. Hadley's award, your family in town, Chase growing up, this case being cold for so many years . . I know I wouldn't survive without knowing who hurt someone I loved. It's the family's closure that's got me like this."

Frankie kneels in front of me on the couch and places her hands on my knees. "I understand this inherited case has been very difficult. You might be on point with your analysis, but I have the reputation and the doctorate. Let me look over everything and put something together for the file. You find the evidence to back up your gut. You never know what you might find. Technology has changed a hell of a lot in the last few years. Shake the old trees. See if anything new falls out."

"I just can't shed this feeling, this hunch."

"I wouldn't expect you to. That makes you a better detective in the long run. All I am asking is that you focus on what you do best. Get the evidence to put him away. Focus on what you can control and allow me to handle what I can, as well." Her calming voice washes over me. "We'll catch him. Your team is too good not to."

Frankie's right. My team is a formidable one, and it's only a matter of time. It's historically accurate and destined to repeat itself.

"I just think . . ."

The taste of her lips on mine surrounds me with a warmth of strength and love. I pull her forward and lean back on the couch. Her heels hit the floor, hands sliding along my sides to the underside of my breasts. Without a doubt this is extremely unprofessional, but for some reason we both become insatiable when intelligence shines through. It's sexy, it's hot, and it stops my brain from processing anything other than our pleasure for the moment.

Chapter Seven

The workday ends with no major breaks in the case and I finish all the paperwork stacked on my desk. Without any further excuses to avoid it, I head to the restaurant to meet Frankie's family for dinner. I'm late, but not terribly so. There's a crowd in the doorway that begrudgingly parts as I step up to the hostess's counter.

"I'm here for a reservation under Ryan," I say.

The hostess looks frazzled and underpaid. She scans the list and stops on the name. "Yes, your party is already here. Follow me."

The line behind me mumbles their irritation at having to wait for the hostess to return. We weave through the tightly packed tables in Times Square's hottest Italian restaurant. The hostess stops and points over to Frankie and Chase, who are laughing. The three other diners sit with their backs to me.

Taking a deep breath, I center myself and head over with all the enthusiasm of a convict heading to the firing squad. I hadn't wanted Chase to be here this evening. I wanted a buffer for him, but then again, maybe he can be one for me. He's innocent. Maybe they will be less likely to rip my head off with a child at the table.

"And you managed to beat that level?" Waylon's deep, raspy voice hits my eardrums.

"Jasmine, you made it!" Frankie's smile brightens the room and immediately puts me at ease.

Wyatt Ryan stands from the table and turns to face me. He struggles with his right leg, the cane he uses to walk just barely out of reach. The six-foot-tall man intimidates with his full head of white hair, solid frame, and piercing blue eyes. His gaze bores holes into my soul as I extend my hand.

"Mr. Ryan," I say, with a slight vibration of my voice.

"Detective." He grasps my hand so tight I feel my index finger knuckle pop into position.

"Daddy . . ." Frankie says with an underlying warning in her tone.

He releases my hand but never breaks eye contact. I look over to the other two men, who are facing forward in their chairs.

"Wade, Waylon it's nice to see you again." They don't even turn around to acknowledge my presence.

"You probably suck at it." Chase's voice rises above the silence, calling my attention.

"Chase, that is not how you speak to your uncles," Frankie says. The word "uncles" grates on my nerves. They're not his uncles, let alone his friends right now. They're simply her brothers until we're married, and even then, that title might never come out of my mouth for them.

"It's okay Frankie, kids, right?" Waylon says. "Wade does suck. He's too busy with his truck to care about gaming." He takes a long pull from his beer bottle. He leans over the table, stabs a ravioli with his fork, and places the entire thing in his mouth, the sauce hitting the end of his full beard and rolling down to the napkin tucked into his collar. His stomach protrudes and hits the table in front of him. His legs manspread a bit to give him more breathing room. He's gained weight since the last time I saw him.

I slink around the table, Mr. Ryan's eyes following my movements I'm sure. Sliding into the bench next to Chase, I kiss the top of his head.

"Aunt Jazz!" He brushes his hands through his hair to brush it off in disgust.

"Still calling you his aunt?" Mr. Ryan asks pointedly.

"It's what I am," I answer, my mother's voice erupting from deep within my chest.

Frankie changes gears to try and defuse the situation. "I ordered the chicken cutlets for you and Chase to share. I know you don't like all the cheese."

"Then why'd we come here? This place screams cheese plus cheese divided by garlic," Wade adds with a slight chuckle. "We could have found a great steak place or maybe some of that sushi stuff you're always tryin' to get me to eat. Claire won't even consider the stuff, but you know me . . ."

"You see food, you eat it," Frankie says. Her eyes are firmly focused on her father.

"Yeah, kids hate it though," Wade says. "Pickiest eaters I've ever met, you know? Casey and Wendall don't eat nothing unless their mother does. Like she's the marker for if it's good or not. I made bacon, and Wendall just stared at it for ten minutes. It was the craziest thing. You figure his sister would grab it, but Mom was at work, so they didn't eat nothing but the toast. Who doesn't like bacon? Am I right?"

"They don't like bacon?" Chase asks Wade with a smile.

"They haven't tried it. I have to wait until we're all together and make it again. Then they'll enjoy it." He smiles back.

I look at Wade and try to convey my appreciation for the change of subject. His physically intimidating muscles, clean-shaven face, piercing green eyes, and military crew cut makes him less approachable for most people. But Frankie's middle brother has always been her teddy bear. She'd be on a video call with me during school, and when we'd fight, he'd remind her how hard relationships are.

He should know though. He and his wife Claire are saddled with each other for eternity, but neither one is truly happy with the other. The one night of passion they shared ended up with a positive stick and two traditional families demanding a wedding. Wade dropped out of college and went to work at the local factory as a supervisor, thanks to his dad. He never talks about Claire's job or if she's happy or not. He's all about his kids and the classic Chevy he's rebuilding.

"Hey, Chase, you like cars?" Wade asks.

"I guess. I'm really good at racing games, but Aunt Jazz doesn't let me drive yet," he says.

"You have a little bit of growing up to do before we give you keys to a car, Chase," Frankie says with a lighthearted lilt to her voice.

"What about Legos, little man?" Wade asks while shoving a piece of steak into his mouth.

"I love Legos! I have a lot of the architecture ones."

"Well, working on cars is just like working with Legos," Wade says. His gaze slides sideways to meet mine. "No matter how much you try, the pieces go together exactly as they're supposed to. You can build what you want, but it's always the same connection. Unless you destroy the foundation of the Lego or the car part, there are literally only two options: connection or disconnection. Just the way God made 'em." He shoves another piece of food in his mouth.

"But aren't all these pieces made out of plastic molds that man creates? And considering that man created them, what stops man from changing them?" Frankie asks Wade.

"Just because man created the mold doesn't mean that it wasn't information handed down from a higher power," Mr. Ryan adds.

"But once again, that higher power has to give the information to man. That man then has to develop, interpret, and process what's been told to him in a way that makes rational sense. In other words, the mold is made based on an idea of the higher power, but is truly more of a picture of the man than the original words," Frankie fires back.

"You sound just like Mom," Waylon says. "Changing the subject . . . maybe Chase and I can get together for a game night while we're here. Can't have the poor kid stuck on certain levels that we could easily beat together."

"I already told you I passed that level," Chase answers. He's oblivious to the tension hovering over the table.

"We have to see what your Uncle Will has planned for the two of you, but I don't see why not," I say, trying to extend an olive branch.

Frankie stares at me, confusion written all over her face. I can't tell if she's happy that I've acquiesced to Waylon's request or irritated. I don't know what she's got planned, but I'm sure a night playing video games is something that we can fit in. Truthfully, I'd prefer if that night included Will. I don't need Chase's head being filled with lies about me or his parents.

"Francesca tells me you're working on a new case," Mr. Ryan says.

"Forgive me, sir, but every day can bring a new case in. Not sure which one she's referring to." I busy myself with cutting up my food.

"Is it the one on the news? The one with the flowers?" Waylon asks. "Heard he's been around for a while. Made the news all the way out in Colorado."

"That's one of them. I can't go into any detail about any of them though. I hope you understand," I say.

"Well, if what the news is saying is true, the victims are all unfaithful women," Wade says.

My anger is rising. "You have a daughter, don't you?" I ask.

"So?" he answers and slightly puffs out his chest.

"What if she was a victim? Assaulted?" I ask.

"My girl wouldn't be one of them. She wouldn't make the mistakes that her mother made. I'm raising her right. She knows her place, she knows her faith, and she knows I don't tolerate any straying from it," Wade says. He leans back in his chair and crosses his arms in front of him for emphasis.

"I understand you're a traditionalist . . ." I start to say.

"I'm sorry. I can't handle this fake family dinner anymore," Wade says and drops the napkin over his plate. "After all that crap she put you through, I can't give you my blessing, Frankie. Truthfully, I don't understand this *relationship* you have. It ain't real, and it ain't right. You don't have to like me for it, but I love you, Frankie, and I'm just trying to save you from yourself."

Wade stands up, grabs his coat from behind the chair, and forcefully moves through the throngs of people and out of sight. Without saying a word, Frankie's father follows suit. Waylon wipes his mouth with his napkin and leans back slightly in his chair. The conflict of whether to stay or go is evident on his face. Chase looks confused and looks back and forth between Frankie and me. I smile and tousle his hair.

"You don't have to stay, Waylon," Frankie says with a shaky voice. One look at her and I can see the unshed tears as she blinks furiously. Her arm wraps tightly around Chase as he continues eating his chicken.

"You know I just want you being happy, Frankie. That's all I've ever wanted. I can't understand your relationship, or what you feel for each other. I only do what Mom taught me to do, and that's to protect my baby sister. I know Dad thinks I'm just a pencil-pushing, lazy, sack of shit teacher, but it doesn't take a lot to know you love Jasmine."

"I do, very much," she says as a few tears escape.

"Dad and Wade will come around. They love you too much not to." Waylon stands and grabs his jacket. "Jasmine, you ever pull that leavin' crap again . . . well, let's just agree that you should never do it again. It's not just about you anymore."

Waylon slips his coat on and meanders through the maze of tables and out the front door. The waiter comes to the table, and I can hear Frankie mumbling to him as he grabs a plate or two to take back to the kitchen. This dinner was supposed to be a family gathering to catch up and laugh together. Instead, it turned into a Thanksgiving meal from hell after a massive political theft of office. Both sides stayed firm in their beliefs, one voted third party because they didn't like any of the other candidates, and one was oblivious and didn't vote. This felt exactly like that.

"Could be worse," I say.

"Are you serious?" Frankie says. She angrily signs the check that her family ran out on.

I watch my fiancée get Chase ready to leave as her hands shake. The waiter hands me the food they wrapped up while my mind was elsewhere. From start to finish, I think it was ten or fifteen minutes before it all went south. If that small amount of time felt like an eternity, I can only imagine what the wedding is going to be like. Unless things quickly change for the better, Frankie is going to get hurt no matter how this situation ends.

When you can't protect the ones you love, the guilt within you grows exponentially. She might lose her biological family if she stays with me. She will lose her chosen family if she doesn't. It's an impossible decision. It's also one she shouldn't have to make. Waylon's right; this isn't about just me anymore. Just like it isn't about them or their beliefs. It's about their little sister being happy. Something they seem to have forgotten.

Chapter Eight

The smell of breakfast hits my nostrils as I get ready for another day. Show tunes flow up the stairs to my ears, along with the melodic voice of my fiancée singing along. As I come downstairs, I see Frankie standing in the doorway of the kitchen, sliding from the stove to the table in her fuzzy slipper socks. Her cellphone and a Bose Bluetooth speaker rest on the counter near the Keurig we use strictly for tea.

I hear her singing: "From now on . . . and we will come back home, and we will come back home, home again!" She continues to sing while putting rice onto both of our plates. She'll never accept the compliment, but her voice is beautiful. She took lessons as a child but stopped when her mother died. She told me it wasn't the same. I never pushed.

Pearl Ryan, Frankie's mom, is something of a mystery to me. She died after a long battle with cancer. I've asked about her medical history, considering it might be hereditary, but Frankie just says the doctors know and that's it. I wish she would open up about it, but I have to be patient. I know the pain of losing a parent, but the idea that what killed her could devour Frankie as well . . . that is a whole different therapy session. I just hope she tells me eventually. I've watched too many people shrivel away and die from disease. I need to know what we might face so I can attempt to prepare myself. Foolish, but still a necessity for my mind to have time to process it.

"What did I do to deserve bacon, eggs, and bacon-fried rice?" I ask.

Frankie spins around and almost loses her balance. "Shit, Jasmine! You scared me."

She puts water in the frying pan and places it back on the stove.

"Sorry, just admiring your voice and the smell of crispy bacon." I sit down in my chair and wait patiently for her to join me.

"Your tea might be lukewarm. I let you sleep a bit longer."

"It is, but I can easily reheat it," I say. "So, why did you make my favorite breakfast? What do you need me to do today?"

"Nothing. Can't I just make some comfort food for my beautiful fiancée for no specific reason?" she asks. She takes a bite of her bacon and begins mixing her food together. Her downcast eyes indicate there is more to it than that.

"You can, but it is a bit out of character." I notice there are only two plates on the table and scan the house. "Frankie, where's Chase?"

"I asked Will to take him for the weekend. He agreed to allow Waylon to come over and have a game night. Before you get upset, I gave him some money for food and snacks. I would like Chase to have a relationship with my family in whatever limited capacity that is. I hope you understand." She takes another bite of food.

"I do, and it's okay. You could have woken me up to let me know or just ask me if I was cool with it. Then I would have been awake to talk about the elephant in the room." I stop eating and place my hand over hers. "Frankie, we promised no secrets."

She sets her fork down before holding onto my hand tightly. "I do want him to know my family. They're my blood, and he could use good people around him. But truthfully, I didn't want him to be around to hear me say things about my family. I don't want him to be jaded because of my thoughts. I want him to make his own opinions."

Her hand grasps mine for support. There's turmoil and pain behind her eyes. The darker rings around her eyes evidence of her lack of sleep from the night before. She's been processing throughout the evening. I can already see she's made a decision.

"I'm going to tell my father and Wade to go home. I don't need their negativity anywhere near me, near us. I get enough of it every day at work. Fuck, I hear all the homophobic bullshit on the news every day. I don't want Chase to be exposed to that kind of rhetoric being directed toward us from people who raised me. It's easy to dismiss evil and cruel people in the world when they aren't related to you. I don't think I could get through explaining how my father and brother hate me for being with the one I love. He's still so innocent . . . I can't do it yet."

"Sweetie, he's been exposed to it. He's already dealt with worse on a slightly smaller scale, right?"

"But not from people who are supposed to love you unconditionally. People like us who raise children and tell them we'll always have their best interests at heart. Not from my daddy . . ." She stops as her voices cracks and tears slowly roll down her face.

I never believed my father loved me. He never expressed it. Frankie's father never let his girl go a day without a kiss on her head or being tucked in at night. He was a cold man, but he loves his little girl.

"Anyway," she continues as water hits her cheeks before she brushes them away. "I've been looking over your Keets case, and I think I have some answers for you."

"I've got your back, Frankie. I don't care what they think. You want us here, we stay. You want us to leave, we'll figure out visitation. The most important thing is for you to be happy. I'll give up everything to ensure that." I squeeze her hand and swallow the dread forming in my chest. "I guess Marlow was busy or Locke just went ahead and called you about this."

"Does it matter?"

"Not really. You were saying?" I shove some eggs in my mouth and force them down with a hard swallow. The bile rushes down my esophagus along with the food into my empty stomach. The pain in it from my anxiety almost forces my body to bend in half. My entire body clenches tightly, fighting itself.

"First, I did look through all the paperwork and attempted to under-stand all the military jargon. Well, what wasn't redacted. I swear there's no point in releasing half of it if you can't read it." She wipes the lingering tears from her face and goes back to eating between words. "The physical evidence does implicate Keets in these murders. That being said, there were some things that didn't sit well with me."

She reaches over to a small pile of papers on the table and pulls out a steno pad. "It's true he exhibited signs of schizophrenia when he re-turned to civilian life. However, he was never given the Rorschach or any other exam for insight into his symptoms. His medical report never even takes his military experiences overseas into account. I've had patients who suffered from PTSD with auditory hallucinations, some visual ones as well. It's not uncommon."

"So, the original doc was wrong or exorbitantly inept?"

"No, I don't like to use the words right or wrong. Everything is some-what subjective without proper testing. I have no idea why the district attorney or anyone in his office didn't notice the glaring errors in the testing. It's shoddy work at least, and in my opinion, criminal to have this pathetic write-up."

"Well, from what I understand, Keets refused all testing."

"A court order would have forced him to comply. The doctor made no attempt to secure one. Even if he didn't, there should have been some references to possible mental issues caused by his actions in the desert."

"Even with that, we both know he would be difficult at best and com-bative at worst. Can someone demand his full jacket be released? I've got wild ideas, but no idea what can actually be done in this case."

"It's a waste of time and resources to try and get all the information about his experiences. They'll claim national security, and it will be de-nied. He could have gotten a hangnail and it would be protected under those same pretenses. We could speak to the rest of his unit, assuming they're back on American soil and available."

"Circles upon circles of red tape."

"Even though they have valid reasons, it's a no-win situation. So, after scouring all of this information, there are areas where the redactions are slightly lighter than others. If I tilt the paper under the light, I can actually make out some snippets of a gunfight and something about children being there. Those words give me enough concern about his mental stability after his tours. Add that to the financials and one could make a case for not guilty by mental disease or defect."

"You know our district attorney refers to that with the same disdain as the Twinkie defense." I smile, sipping my tea.

"Yes, well, there was an uproar when Hostess went out of business, but that isn't the case here. Sugar or lack thereof didn't cause him to murder his family. Seeing a child bleed out in the middle of a sandy dune might. Especially if you wonder whose bullet took their life — yours or theirs. Either way, if you weren't there, would this child have died? Those questions can cripple a normal human being, but with the visuals of war . . . I would imagine his attorneys know all of this. I'm surprised you didn't come right out and tell Locke this information."

"Giving her the number to our FBI contact and permission to call your office was already asking for trouble. I don't need another case being pulled aside or having my name splashed in the press. I just wanted to focus on my own to-do list, ya know?" I chug some of my cooler tea to continue pressing the pain down. "I suspected some of what you said, but I also know people lie through their teeth to get out of serving time. Malingerers do exist, and they fuck up the history of a decent science."

"Well, now that I've gotten involved, I have to go to the prosecution with this. Your name will come up."

"I was never truly attached to it. Will's handling the office side, so you can work with him on it. Contact Major General Dennis Carter. For whatever reason, he decided to interject himself into a case that wasn't his concern. He owes me one, so use my 'get some information free' card."

"That might not go over well."

"Maybe not, but it's also possible that he's not so bad a guy. He might have been doing what he thought was right, even if it did complicate things. I know the government needs to stay out of our way until they have evidence proving they need to be involved. If you do talk to him, maybe suggest that? I think Marlow's sick of me texting her my complaints," I say, finishing up my last piece of bacon before placing the silverware on the plate.

"I'll make some calls, but Will's with Chase and Waylon."

"If you trust your brother, then I guess I'll have to trust him alone with Chase for a little bit." My cell phone begins to rattle across the table. "Steele."

Frankie takes her last bite, stands, and begins clearing off the table. I watch her closely as the captain rattles off more information in my ear. She fills the dishwasher, catches the expression on my face, and abruptly stops everything.

"What's wrong?" she mouths to me.

"Are you sure?" I ask meekly. "I'll be there."

I disconnect the call, jump to my feet, and scan the room for my car keys.

"Jasmine?" She tries to get my attention, but I continue to look around for keys that should be near the door.

"Sweetheart?"

"Do you know where my keys are?"

"On the hook by the door where you always put them." She's right; they're hanging next to all the keys on the hinge side of the door. "Are you going to tell me what's going on?"

"I need you to watch Chase and work with Will on the Keets case, please." The nerves rolling down my spine come out in the shakiness of my voice.

"I will. Now tell me what's got you so worked up."

"Someone just walked into the station asking to speak with me." I turn to face Frankie. "He says I've been looking for him. If he's the killer, why would he do that? I mean . . . he's gotten away with it for so long, why come to me now?"

"Sure it's not a prank?"

"Zeile doesn't seem to think so. Says the guy is willing to give proof but will only talk to me."

"Jesus."

Frankie dries her hands on a rag quickly before grabbing her phone, keys, and jacket. "You get to the precinct, and I'll get the profile. This action might fit if we look at the bigger picture. If it's a challenge to you and the team, he's raising the stakes a bit. You said it yourself; he's gotten away with it for so long, there must be a reason. Maybe he wants more of a rush?" She pushes me out the door. "Go do what you do best. I'll call you if I have anything."

"Be safe."

"I'll have Will work the military angle from there as well. Come home to me." I kiss her and slam the door behind me.

Sitting in my car waiting for it to warm up, my stomach churns with the negative anxiety that I managed to keep in check throughout breakfast. The unknowns and the questions roll around in my head like the balls on a billiards table after a break. If he is the killer and we fail to show enough cause to charge him, he could walk out a free man. Everything that comes after will be on my shoulders and mine alone.

***

From the depths of the parking garage, I take the elevator to the main floor of the precinct. It's somewhat of a surreal experience. Officers stand with their backs to me, bringing to life the figurative phrase "wall of blue." Cameras flash and record my every step from the main lobby as reporters scream questions. I spy Zeile on the other side of the crowd, and I head toward him. Several plainclothes detectives look at me, some with disdain and others with valid concern. I may have just been handed this case on a silver platter, or it could destroy my career. And then there are the lives of countless future victims. Nothing to worry about.

"Detective, if you'll follow me, please," Captain Zeile says.

Once we're out of earshot, I whisper, "You okay?"

"Let's get to your office, shall we?"

He clears a path through the throng of detectives and officers milling around the front area. The congestion might look good in images or video, but overall, it's a smokescreen. It's never this crowded up front.

Walking into my office, I see one person standing in the middle of the room—someone who shouldn't be here, let alone be allowed in during this ruckus.

"Sir?"

"You have five minutes while our other visitor goes through the proper security processes." He holds up five fingers to emphasize his point before heading into his office. I close the door, blocking out the sound beyond the walls.

"Frankie know you're here?"

"No, she called me and canceled lunch. Busy case."

"I'll call her." My hands fumble with my cell phone in my jacket pocket.

"Don't." Mr. Ryan gently lifts the photo of Frankie, Chase, and me off my desk, his calloused hand tracing the outlines of all of our faces. His eyes have a longing in them buried beneath the saddlebags of time. "She's like her mother. Needs to stay focused on tasks at hand. It's easier than feeling out of control."

"She's also an in-demand professional. Frankie's busy because she is one of the best criminal psychologists in this city. She chooses to help people, even if it means time away from her family, because it's the right thing to do. It's what she feels she needs to do," I say. If he wants to attack me that's fine, but Frankie is off-limits.

"You get awfully protective of her," he says with a slight drawl to his words. "Ever think her keeping busy was a compliment? Pearl was the same way. Everyone loved her, needed her help with one thing or another. She was the best kindergarten teacher; won awards too. The stress of helping out the kids who had nothing, fighting the idiots who sit at a desk . . ." He pauses, and I hear him take a deep breath as he places the frame back in its original location. "It broke her more times than I could fix, I guess. Cancer just did the rest."

He pushes off my desk and walks right up to me, worn eyes staring through me.

"I don't know what she sees in ya. I don't know why she is the way she is. I'm sure she could find a good man to spend the rest of her life with." He stops and continues his long, deep breathing as if trying to find the words to say next.

Part of me wants to fire back words of anger about not being able to choose who you love, but I stand frozen to the spot, more out of respect for Frankie than anything else. Sometimes it's the hardest thing a human being can do—be silent.

"God help me, she loves you. And God help me . . . I love my daughter, and that nephew of yours makes me laugh like I haven't in ages." He chuckles slightly before his face morphs into a significantly scary-serious one. "You break her heart again and I swear to God they'll never find your body. Understand me?"

I'm stunned. I don't know what to do, so I nod. He pats me on the shoulder and moves past me. "Don't worry about Wade. He's just a little shit that needs guidance. I'll handle him. Might take a while, but I'll handle him."

He finishes his statement and slowly makes his way out of my office with his cane. If I weren't an adult, I would have wet myself. That man and his family are old-school, hard-working people that know how to scare the bejesus out of you with one look. I have no doubt in my mind that Frankie would never find the body.

"Steele?"

I hear the captain's voice behind me, pulling me back to the task at hand. I fix my shirt collar, crack my neck, and exhale. I turn and head into the dungeon.

"What do we know?"

"Nothing much. He walked in and said he knew you and would like to speak with you about the Carnation Killer case. When pressed, the admitting officer states he refused to give more information unless you were present. Office assumes he's the killer," Zeile answers.

"Exact words?" I press.

"Nope, and nothing on tape or written. That's why you need to get a confession out of him. Otherwise, we have twenty-four hours to either charge him or let him go."

"Get a court order for his DNA immediately."

"Already on it. Dr. Brown said the test would take one to two days regardless. He'll be out the door by then."

"We sure this isn't a crank?"

"I don't think so, but you go into that room and give me your impression. You've been attached to this case; you'd know it right away." I lock eyes with him and reach for my phone.

"Logan," I say. "I need you to talk to the captain, get all the information you have, and do as much digging as you can." I hand my cell to Zeile as I remove my gun and place it in my desk drawer. "I can't go in there looking for a fight. It's conversational, and you'll be watching the whole time."

"His name's—"

"Don't tell me. Conversational, introductions, and all. Just make sure you're recording. Give Logan access to the feed and see if you can get Dr. Ryan in to watch somehow. Maybe they can see something we can't."

I hear the captain talking to Logan and some loud music in the background. Oh shit. Logan's with Hadley. Dammit—she has the closing ceremonies of the festival tonight. She's still upset I left early, even if she says she understands. At least I think she does; if she hasn't called to yell at me, I'm usually in the clear. She's been doing some press for the new film and awards season. Even Logan's been pissy about lack of girlfriend time.

Right now, though, I need to win an acting award of my own. Considering he came in two hours ago, I have approximately twenty-two more to figure out who he is, what he wants, and if he's actually our guy. I don't know which is worse: hunting down the killer or playing a game of roulette with the lives of future victims. Twenty-two hours. I crack my neck one more time and walk into the interview room.

Chapter Nine

The interview room is the same cold, nondescript room in every police station. There's cement, gray walls, two chairs, and a metal table in the middle, bolted to the floor. A White male of average build sits perfectly upright in one of the metal chairs, his hands clasped together in handcuffs, resting on top of something. He remains steadfast, looking forward as if he can see Captain Zeile through the one-way mirror. The door's hinges screech as I close it and walk into the unknown.

"I'm sorry to keep you waiting." I grab the chair and sit across from the man. His eyes are unflinching on their constant focal point. "My name is Detective St—"

"Detective Jasmine Steele holds a John Jay College of Criminal Justice Masters of Forensic Psychology degree. I saw your talk on the Carnation Killer. It was rather informative, although slightly misguided."

His calm demeanor sends a slight chill up my spine. Slowly, his dark eyes slide down the wall, over the table, and up my torso until they lock onto mine. Facial hair has begun to grow on his jawline, maybe a day or two's worth.

"You like it?" he says as my eyes dart over his face in search of recognition. His cold grin is something I've never witnessed in my entire career. It's calculated, designed to get a response. It pushes my entire body back in the chair without a verbal or physical threat. "I've never had one before. Now is as good a time as any, don't you think?"

"If that is your sort of thing, I don't see why not," I mindlessly answer.

"Ah yes. You prefer the fairer sex, like Dr. Ryan. My apologies for not properly presenting myself." He continues to smile his sadistic grin. I feel the goose bumps rising on my arms, thankful for the long-sleeved button-down I grabbed this morning. "You do have exquisite taste."

"Yes, thank you."

His head is perfectly shaved. No tattoos are visible on his neck or wrists. No earrings. Never grew his facial hair out before. I rack my brain, trying to remember all the faces that crossed my path during the conference. Nerves and discomfort make everything blur together until the face of the man in front of me comes into view. The one who questioned my abilities. The professor.

"Forgive me. I don't remember your name."

"You wouldn't know it, as I never gave it. Karl Schlect. My business associate, Mr. Brandy, said you were looking for me. Dreamers Den," he adds.

"I appreciate you coming in."

"You felt technology would catch this killer of yours. Do you still feel this is the case?" His questions quickly push me into a defensive posture. "I think anything is possible with the proper team in place."

"Yes, Detective Locke is a new addition to the team. Hardheaded and steadfast. An interesting counterpoint to you, don't you think?"

My expression must give me away, because he spins the newspaper from the captain's office around so I can read it. "I was allowed to keep it. The worst it could give you is a paper cut, detective. Interesting reading though." He flips to the article, and there's a picture of Locke and me leaving the crime scene. "The media are fickle, aren't they? One minute you're everyone's darling, but the next minute they hang this murder around your inability to solve a case."

"I don't work for them."

"Very true, you work for the taxpaying public of this city. Which I happen to be a resident of." He leans back in his chair, letting the paper rest between us. "You're quoted as saying that the killer was a 'narcissistic limp dick who needs to get off on hurting women.' Rather out of character for a woman of your standing, isn't it?"

"I do believe this individual might have some psychological issues, yes." My voice is firm but emotionless. My mind is running a mile a minute. That smug voice. Where have I heard it . . .?

At the conference. The man who confronted me and tried to bait me into an argument at the time. He almost succeeded, but Frankie pulled me away from it. Is this the man we've been looking for or just the true crime enthusiast he claims to be? "You would know the context of my statement best, wouldn't you?"

"And the prodigal child remembers." His smile finally reaches his eyes, but it's eerie and seems more like a jeering clown's. "Before you ask, no, I didn't write this, nor did I make a call to a reporter. No, see, your voice carries to the rafters and beyond. Your fiancée tried to keep it down, but you kept going. So, now the metro area knows of your challenge and disdain for the man."

"I appreciate you coming in, but do you have anything to add to this investigation?"

"Well, anything to assist one of our more famous alumni! The infallible Jasmine Steele of John Jay College." His arms hang straight across the table as he slowly claps.

"That's not accurate."

"Which part?" He stops clapping. His hands rest on the table, thumbs pressing hard into the metal.

"I'm just doing my job. Now, is there anything—"

"Modesty doesn't suit you, Jasmine. We both know you're much more secure in yourself than that. Please don't play the self-deprecating detective with me. It's insulting." Schlect pulls his hands back and folds them on his lap. He's emotionless and almost too calm. He shows no signs of discomfort in a room with the heat a bit higher than normal. His skin is pale, not flushed or showing signs of nervous sweat. His voice has been a normal timbre throughout this entire conversation. He's a psychopath.

I know I've given away my understanding of the situation because the creepy clown smile returns to his face. He's showing me the game board, but he has pieces in play everywhere, risking every smaller or inconsequential piece to lure me in that direction. Anything to win. Frankie's words radiate through my mind all at once. He is here to take back whatever power or notoriety he feels I've taken from him.

"Now that we have an understanding, please ask your questions." He sits up in a perfect right angle, crosses his left leg over his right, and places his clasped hands on his knee.

"We have evidence that a few women were last seen in your bar the day they died." It's a statement rather than a question. More of a fuck you to Schlect for giving me permission to do my job.

"It is a popular destination for single women, students, and other living, breathing individuals," he counters.

"We would need to know everything you know—video surveillance or credit card receipts."

"You don't need those things." A small smile creeps across his face.

"We're trying to pinpoint the exact time of abduction or—"

"You know what the white carnation stands for?" he asks.

"In high school, they gave out white carnations for a secret admirer."

"What school? Parochial or public"

"Catholic. Does this really matter?"

"Pity to be denied a proper education for the means of a watered-down book of man's interpretation of the truth and the light."

"Mr. Schlect—"

"Karl. We're both on the same plane, Jasmine." His gaze slides above me to the glass for a few seconds before returning to mine. "Ich kenne Sie." His perfect German accent rolls off his tongue, filling the room. The translation of I know you, causes a rippling of discomfort up my spine.

"Karl," I say, planning my next move. No one outside of my core friends knows I speak German. He's trying to keep this between him and me. A power play. If I follow suit, he wins the move, but he also might be more open to speaking honestly. If I refuse to acknowledge his lead, it might be an insult and he could walk out the door. I choose to be upfront and ask if he was the killer. *"Hast du diese Frauen getötet?"*

His laughter bounces off the walls, reaching my ears in surround sound. As quickly as it begins, it stops. His face falls back into the stoic, blank expression that hides all the bits of information I need. "You should know better than to ask that," he answers in English. "Your mother taught you well. The accent is flawless."

"Grandmother," I counter. "I'll ask again. Did you kill those women?"

"The white carnation symbolizes purity and luck. Using the white carnations as a secret admirer in your Catholic school is interesting." He's running me in circles with no direct north. "What does that mean to you, Jasmine?"

"It's a flower."

"Oh, come now, you're smarter than that. Why would a person leave something that means purity and good luck on a body? You've spoken to crowds and the press about the crime scenes, the fact that the flower was in full bloom, the heart carved just above it. Why would someone do that?" he presses.

I never got my doctorate, and I've never been expert enough to discuss things like this. Frankie would be the better option, but I'm cornered.

"Since you were also at my talk, you would remember he washed their bodies clean." He closes his eyes and inhales. It's like he's remembering. "One could infer that he was making them pure and clean for the afterlife. The carnation is the ultimate symbol of it."

He looks me in the eyes. *"Es ist pure schönheit."*

"What's pure beauty?" I ask. I'm hoping he sticks with English. I need those behind the glass to be able to follow the more important parts.

"The flower: perfect, untainted, clean of chemicals and dyes. It's practically untouched as God intended. You understand."

"The bodies . . . prepared for the world beyond the veil."

"Possibly. Maybe that's what the killer wants. That would make sense if that was what *really* mattered, but is it?"

"I think it's a mix of both wielding power and relinquishing it at the same time."

"Intriguing sentiment, but how do you suppose someone as powerful as your killer would be able to let go of all that strength he wields?" He raises his eyebrows at me, a smile slowly creeping across his face. I resist the urge to shudder.

"It's a balance." I take a deep breath and channel my internal analysis computer to work double-time. "The victims are all women looking for some connection, if only for a night. The Carnation Killer seems to long for the same thing, but he needs control over the entire event. Once their life is taken, there is a release of control. The body is cleaned . . . prepared for the police to find later. It's a strategic game of sorts. He puts a piece on the board as he wishes it to be found and we must interpret it. But he no longer has control over the situation. I do."

"Or he relinquishes control to God and his judgment of the released soul," he says. "As you said, the flower could exemplify this very clearly."

His meanderings are wasting my time. He's made his first move on the board. Time for a counter that brings him back to reality.

"The organic compounds we found in the flowers were still created by man. Not really pure there, Karl. So, the message would be lost in the scientific breakdown. If you have information . . . "

"Interesting thought." He leans forward, his elbows resting on the table and his eyes scanning over my entire body. "But not unexpected."

"You came to see me, Karl. Can you help us or not?"

He quickly spins out of his chair. Him standing over me is meant to be oppressive. The laughter pours out of his mouth like venom, spraying and bouncing off the walls. The feeling burns through my soul to nerves of steel I pretend to have.

"I have been helping you, but you haven't been paying attention."

"No, Schlect. I've been listing to the ramblings of a man trying to be relevant to me. I'm not indulging you anymore." I stand up and walk to the door and rap twice. It swings inward. "*Schönen Tag noch*," I say before slamming the door behind me.

***

I walk back into the captain's office and see Frankie standing at the glass. She has an expression on her face I can't read. Captain Zeile looks over at me and hits a button on the wall, which cuts off the sound from the other room.

"What did you say to him?" she asks.

"Have a good day."

"Why would you say that? We don't want him to leave!" Captain Zeile raises his voice.

"He won't," Frankie interjects. "She dismissed him. A dangerous move."

Frankie looks me over before leaning back against the one-way mirror. I can tell thoughts are running rampant in her mind as she tries to connect the dots. One thing I know for sure is the killer is sitting in our interrogation room. Twenty-one hours until release. We're running out of time.

"Have Logan dig up everything he can on Karl Schlect. I'm heading over to my alma mater to see if they have anything on him. When we met, he mentioned teaching psychology classes for undergraduates and graduates at John Jay. I think it's time to raid his office and see what information his associates can give us."

"You broke through the first layer, Jasmine, but you're going to need much more to break him," Frankie says. In the interrogation room, Karl's eyes are locked on the glass. "He really gives me the creeps."

"What do you think? Is he our guy?" Zeile asks. The two of us nod in agreement. "Then you do what you have to and let me figure out a way to hold him."

"Hold him on old parking tickets until you can garner up enough evidence for the charges you want," Frankie tosses out.

"Honey, while I appreciate the sentiment, you've worked here long enough to know we don't just do that. It's a bit more complicated than that."

"I know. But desperate times . . ." she finishes.

"Get going; I'll talk to Logan and call Xavier ahead of time. The president of John Jay . . . we happen to know one another." He pauses, holding the phone in his hand. "Full resources available, understand?" Zeile looks at me.

"Yes, sir."

I turn to look at the glass one more time. Schlect is still in his chair, legs crossed, with perfect posture and his hands clasped on his knees. He continues to stare at the glass, but there is a small shimmer on his forehead. We've managed to break the façade a little bit. Now we have to shatter it.

***

At any other time, walking down the hallways of my old college would bring a smile to my face. Knowing the truth behind my visit makes me less eager to look around or chat up some former professors. I feel more like breaking hallway etiquette and running as fast as possible to the principal's office.

In the plain, white office, a simple wooden desk sits off to the left of the door. A young male sits behind it.

"Excuse me," I say.

"Can I help you?" he asks.

"I'm here to see President Dorsey. I'm Detective Steele." I flash my badge.

"You can go on in. He's expecting you. Can I get you something to drink?"

"No, thank you," I say and knock on the door before opening it.

Xavier Dorsey, retired FBI agent and now president of the school we nicknamed Terrorism U, stands, holding onto the desk for support, his belly sticking out well beyond his belt line. The images on the wall behind him boast of a prolific career, with various awards and connections made throughout his time. Each image showcases a fit, muscular man that contrasts the man sitting behind the chair.

He trudges slowly, his right leg slightly dragging across the carpet as he steps. Closing the door behind me, I meet him halfway. He reaches with his left hand for a firm handshake.

"Bullet to the spine. The right one doesn't work too well anymore," Xavier says before dragging himself back to his chair.

"I'm sorry . . ."

"It's fine." He slides into his chair, using the desk as support. "You didn't make a negative comment, so you fall into one of two groups: the ones who just stare, never ask, and try to look away, or the ones who analyze my every move, trying to figure it out. Considering your background, I'm guessing the latter."

"Sir . . ."

"Take a seat, detective. I know you're here to talk about Mr. Schlect, but I prefer to look you in the eye without contorting my neck into awkward positions." With his left hand, the president gestures toward the two empty chairs in front of him.

"Sir, I understand Schlect was on staff here. Could you tell me if he had any complaints during his tenure?" I say as I slip into the seat.

"Well, I've been here for three years now, so I wasn't privy to anything out of the ordinary. I've looked through his file and didn't see anything of note. He had a high passing rate, and his reviews at the end of the terms all seem above average."

"Would you have a list of students or other instructors he talks to . . ." I begin.

"Detective, you know I can't just turn over a list to you. He hasn't even been arrested. We pride ourselves on protecting our students and faculty from prying eyes. If there is something to be investigated, tell me now and I will take this matter to the union."

I decide to try another tack. "Did Mr. Schlect oversee any after-school activities? Extra hours? Anything additional to the requirements of being a professor here?"

"Nothing that isn't readily available for you to find on Google."

"Would you allow me access to his office?"

"Not without a warrant." He leans forward in his chair, both elbows firmly on the oak desk. "Now, detective, you might be a highly regarded alumnus here, but you haven't answered my question."

"It's because I can't, sir. Everything is ongoing. You know how that is."

"I do." He leans back and shifts in his chair. His face contorts before settling back into an unreadable gaze. "I also know when you could be wasting all of our time searching for something that isn't there. I assume you can show yourself out."

"Thank you for your time." My words bounce off the door as I close it behind me.

"You should check out the bar," the young student says to me. His floppy brown hair covers his right eye as he leans further over his desk. "The president won't want me telling you this, but Mr. Schlect runs the bar Dreamers Den. He'd give you drinks if you're lucky."

"Underage?"

He nods while staring at the door behind him. I doubt it would move without us hearing the president struggling to reach us.

"Why are you telling me this? Did he do something to you?"

"No . . ." He leans back, moves his hair out of his face as his eyes dart past me.

"I don't give a shit what it is. I just want to know what I'm getting into." My tone is low so as to not raise suspicion.

"He slept with Zaria. I was so close to asking her out and he just, bam, nails it."

"Right. How old is she?"

"Twenty."

"Student?"

"Not in his class. She came with me to the bar one night. Thought it would help me loosen up a bit."

"She got drinks and you didn't." He nods again, but his eyes fall to the desk, causing his hair to obstruct his face. I lean over the desk. "Listen, kid, you and your friends better watch your asses. You don't want to be caught. It might cost you more than you think."

I walk out of the room without waiting to hear another word out of him. I can hear the whimpering echo down the hallway as the realization of what I said sinks in. He's scared shitless that I'm going to rat him out, but I won't do anything. He didn't ply anyone with drinks or harm anyone. He was just willfully stupid. I was that age once—totally vanilla, straightlaced, never drank—but I was that ignorantly youthful.

Dreamers Den smells like a rank old bar. The stale odor of beer filters through the air more than the testosterone from older men hitting on the younger college students. It's pathetic, it's disgusting and, in some cases, illegal.

"Detective, what brings you by? Can I get you a drink?" Shawn asks as he ushers me in and away from the patrons sitting at his tables.

"No, thank you. You're open early."

"It's the weekend. If we're not open, we're not making money," he answers quickly. "Besides, it's almost noon. It's early lunch for the crowds in the area."

"It's noon," I say more to myself than anyone else. Sixteen hours until Schlect's release. I've lost more time than I thought. "Karl Schlect. Start talking."

"Karl? Did you get to talk to him? I told you. I'm not blowing up his spot just cause you—"

My hands are around his shirt collar before I can stop myself. "I'm not here to be nice, asshole. I need information, and you either give it to me or I toss your ass in a cell for obstruction. Or serving minors."

He taps my hand and fixes his shirt quickly. He walks over to one of his staff and whispers something in their ear. He tilts his head at me and moves through the small crowd of patrons. I follow him; some people look at the badge attached to my belt and then up at me. One male grabs the drink in front of his young female companion. He smiles and sips it, pretending both beverages on the table are his. A simple bottle of beer and a bright blue fruit drink. They don't really taste well together, and his scowl shows his disdain.

"Word to the wise, prisoners have a serious disdain for pedophiles. You ply her with liquor, have your way with her, and you'll be labeled," I whisper to the table so only the two of them hear me.

"I'm legal," the girl says. A bright yellow paper bracelet adorns her right wrist. "Eighteen." Young freshman, probably the first time in the big city, thinking she can handle the world. All she sees are bright lights and people being nice. I see the underbelly below all the supposed acts of kindness. Her naivete of her invincibility could be her downfall if she doesn't wise up to reality.

"You might be, kiddo, but if he gets you drunk you can't give consent, and he'll get labeled."

"By who?" she questions.

"Whoever puts him in lockup," I answer.

The man continues to force both drinks down his throat. One gulp of blue sweetness followed by his beer chaser. With every sip, I can see his face contort. Karma is such a wonderful beast. If I had more time, I'd stay to ensure every last sugary drop makes it past his lips. Instead, I smile at the two of them before walking into Shawn's office in the back. I have bigger issues at hand.

It's sparsely decorated: one desk, one computer, a file cabinet, gray walls, and a flickering set of fluorescent lights above. Nothing seems used. It's covered in a layer of dust so thick I could write in it. It's dated, it smells, and they obviously haven't spent any money or time in here.

"What do you want?"

"I told you, I want to know everything about Schlect. Violent? Controlling? Anything odd or strange I should know about him?" I say, looking around the small office for clues.

"Man's smart as hell. Like photographic memory smart. We grew up together in Garden City; he sold his parents' house a year or so ago. Still drives by to see what the new owners have done to the place. He wasn't thrilled with the recent renovation," Shawn mutters quickly. "He's got a dark streak in him, but nothing I haven't seen before."

"How dark? Has he hurt anyone in front of you?" I ask, my attention fully on him.

"Well, he would have these moments when he would mumble shit to himself. Like after he messed up on the baseball field or failed a test. Had a bunch of those moments in college too. He'd just start punching himself in the head while talking to himself." Brandy must feel he's said too much because his eyes widen and his stance changes to a more protective posture. "But he got that all worked out. No meds, nothing. Went to the gym, ate right, graduated with honors . . ."

"You can't cure mental illness with vitamins, proper diet, and exercise. You need significant psychological help. I promise you if he was sick then and was never seen by a doctor, he's still sick. He might have found a way to cope with it that you don't know about." I try to refocus the conversation. "Why did you go into business with him?"

"I was struggling. We were deep in the red. He came in one day with all these great ideas to get people in here."

"Like selling to minors?"

"No. I lowered the age for entry, but those who aren't drinking age get bracelets. If the bartender sees a yellow one, he can't pour. It's simple: pour to a minor and they're shown the door. I don't joke about that," he says quickly.

"I walked in the door and saw several of your clientele buying drinks for much younger girls."

"We can't legislate morality here, detective. I can only do so much."

"Maybe, but pandering to the males in the area who would love to date a younger woman to deflower her? Now, that's an interesting sales pitch."

"We run ladies' nights and other single events. The college kids don't keep us in business; otherwise I wouldn't have needed him to buy into the bar in the first place!" He raises his voice as he steps forward, invading my personal space.

"How did a professor at a city university have enough money to invest in your bar? It's not like they're sitting on piles of cash."

Shawn backs up and turns around in the small space before dropping into the only chair in the room. A puff of dust rises from his action; if I stay much longer, my allergies will make themselves known.

"He got some money from his mom's inheritance. Told me he wanted to help me out since he had a stable income."

"When did she die?"

"Five or six years ago. Something to do with her heart."

"Anything else you want to share?"

He leans back in the chair, quiet. I'm sure I could wrangle more out of him, but it would take more time than I've got. I turn and grab the doorknob but stop.

"If you think of anything else, let me know. Keep better tabs on your customers and bartenders. They keep pulling the same shit, I'll shut you down and throw you in jail. Consider this your one and only warning." I turn the knob and stroll through the bar, looking at the older patrons, almost begging them to say something.

The male from before is gone, but the young freshman is in the corner with some other girls. I don't know why anyone would come to a bar to study, but there are books on the table for the illusion if nothing else. Innocence oozes off them like an aphrodisiac to single men and women. Hopefully they'll be wise enough to protect themselves.

I pray to whatever is out there that I raise Chase to be as respectful as possible. He's going to be headstrong like his father, smart like his mother, and willful like me. Frankie might be the only one able to reel him in, but I don't want him to be caught off guard. The word *no* is powerful, and he has to understand that. I don't care if he's in trouble for doing the right thing. I'd rather bail him out for defending a woman than for abusing her.

Chapter Ten

The drive back to the precinct during the lunch rush was nothing compared to the foot traffic outside the doors. The gaggle of reporters stand with their backs to the doors, mouths moving a mile a minute relaying information to a waiting public. Cameramen holding heavy equipment on slightly sagging shoulders record the feeds. There are vans scattered along the street, a mobile command center for each one of the news crews who litter the area like confetti in Times Square on New Year's Eve.

Every human being that walks by is scanned, assessed for their importance, and some are assaulted with questions. The probation officers walk through, their heads down and mouths shut, their facial expressions almost begging to be left alone. They're not experienced enough to know the way around the wall of bullshit. It's an art that you hone after years of dealing with this inconvenience. The media is our friend when we need it, but also parasitic when we don't.

"Detective Steele." A female reporter calls my name as I try to maneuver through the throngs of people. "Is it true the Carnation Killer turned himself in?" she continues as flashes of light blind my vision.

"No comment." I use my right hand in front of my body, carefully moving through the zombie horde of reporters.

"Does the police department have evidence connecting this man to the murders?" another reporter calls out over the other voices.

"No comment. If you'll excuse me." I continue to push my way to the metal barricade that seems to be holding the swarm back. It's working as well using as a fork to eat soup. No officers are manning the perimeter, just these flimsy metal barriers that anyone can move.

"Back up!" I hear Will's voice bellow over the masses. "Come on, people. Behind the barricades!"

A strong hand grabs my arm and gently pulls me forward. I can hear more questions being thrown at me, blending together in the background. The metal gate screeches against the concrete as I open it. Several uniformed officers file out, finally taking positions along the boundary. The screaming voices of the media fade as we walk into the front hall of the precinct.

"Thanks for the assist," I say, pawing at my face to rub the flashes out of my vision.

"All good. Figured a little lady like you would need help," Will says with a slight laugh.

"Hey, I was fine until the camera flashed like the fucking sun. What the hell was up with all of that?"

"Doing their job," he says. "You good?"

"Yeah. Where's the captain?" I ask.

"Conference room, waiting on us. Shit hit the fan. Come on."

I look back at the growing media presence beyond the small glass doorway. The amount of people out there leads me to believe there was a leak somewhere within these walls. Either that or Schlect set something in motion before showing up here. No matter what the reason, the spotlight on this precinct isn't going to make the higher-ups too thrilled. That alone will put my captain on edge, which means the rest of us are fucked.

"Steele, come on."

Jumping up the three stairs to the main floor landing, I follow Will to the conference room. The rest of the precinct continues to move about at a normal speed. That's a good sign to me, the normalcy of most officers' speed from point A to point B. Will looks at me surveying the room.

"It's all for show," he says. "Captain put a ton of guys on scut work to look busy. Filing papers, entering forms into the new computer systems, anything to look like everything is normal here. The cap even brought in extra officers so we look fully staffed. It's all a pretty elaborate con."

"I'm not surprised. It's a smart play considering how people will believe what they see more than the reality of statistics, reports, or, you know, reality. The general population has an issue with wrapping their brains around things they can't conceptually understand. It's not that they're dumb; they just prefer to ignore what's in front of them than actually face a terrifying prospect. It makes perfect sense."

"I wouldn't go that far, but it's easier to put faith in abstracts than take responsibility. I learned that when I was five. It's why the US is a sue-happy country and billionaires get wealthier by the second."

"And you call me cynical?" I say. I turn to look him in the eyes and stop at the conference room doors.

"Not cynical, a realist. We see the underbelly every day. They"—he tilts his head toward the lobby—"don't. They see it after we clean it up so it doesn't rile the population into a frenzy." He pulls open the heavy wood door leading into the conference room.

The two of us walk inside the already tension-filled room. Captain Zeile stands by the window, his suit jacket resting on the back of a chair. His voice is low, but his tone is deep, almost defensive, as he talks on his cell phone. He holds a coffee that sloshes with each aggressive wave of his hand as the conversation continues.

Sydney sits at the table, a foot-high stack of papers in front of her. She scribbles notes across a small scrap of paper as her other hand slides pages around in seemingly random order.

Major General Carter stands at attention with his guards. Will walks up to them and shakes hands, and they talk in a low mumble I can't quite decipher.

At the other end of the table, Logan sits with Frankie, his head buried in his laptop screen while his cell phone lights up every few seconds. His eyes dart back and forth when it does, like someone staring at a train moving by.

"You look overwhelmed." Frankie's voice hits my ears.

Her suit jacket is open, her hair down and slightly out of place. Her heels rest to the right of her chair. She looks stressed as she sips her tea.

"How bad?"

"Depends on which case you're referring to," she says softly. "One isn't good and one is pure shit."

"I understand!" The captain's voice echoes through the room. He disconnects his phone and squeezes it tightly. I can tell he wants to throw it, or anything he can grab, somewhere. I know that kind of frustration. He turns, places both his hands flat on the table, and stares at me. "Steele, please tell me you found out something."

"I wish I did. President won't release information other than he has no complaints. Shawn Brandy, his business partner, says he was a good guy looking to help a friend out when his mother died. Said he might have some anger issues, but without evidence to back that up, it's all conjecture. They appear to serve alcohol to minors, but we don't have time to get the evidence to hold it over his head regardless of my threats." I look around the room. "Anyone else?"

"You threatened him?" Zeile stares at me, a small vein showing on his forehead.

"Maybe threatened is a strong word. I just advised him in a strong fashion that he needs to watch his employees."

Zeile runs his hands along his neck, trying to rub the tension away. "Please tell me we have a lead." The room is silent, causing the hair on the back of my neck to rise in alarm. "He can't be this clean. Logan? Money? Paper trail from his mother's inheritance? Social media? Anything?"

"I looked everywhere," Logan says. "His accounts are normal for someone in his position, the inheritance from his mother a few years ago, and the subsequent sale of the house. That's it. No parking tickets, no outstanding debts or warrants. Literally he is as off the grid as one can be without disconnecting from society."

"Profile? Anything we can use?" I look over to Frankie.

"Professionally, he fits the profile of a psychopath. He has urges to be the most powerful in any given situation depending on who he attaches himself to. You said he put money into his friend's bar?" I nod in response. "That fits. The file says the most recent victim was last seen there. Maybe it's his hunting ground? If nothing else, it gives him power over his friend."

"So he can move freely because Shawn won't question his motives," Sydney adds.

"Exactly."

"But there was no connection to the bar with the other victims. Just the one," Logan adds.

"Can we please talk about the bigger issue at hand?" Carter says loudly.

"A serial killer walks into our precinct and that isn't the bigger issue?" I ask coldly.

"Not when a man committed suicide while in our custody," Zeile says softly.

The room quiets, all attention on him waiting for more information. He turns, places his phone on the table, and loosens his tie.

"Douglas Keets was found hanging in his cell this morning. He tied the bedsheet around his neck and attached it to the bars."

"How? The walls are solid; only the doors have metal bars. You can't get high enough, and the surveillance—"

"You shorten it enough so you just sit down and asphyxiate yourself," Frankie says. "I've seen it in person. In my opinion, it takes more determination to do it that way. You can easily get up and out of your predicament."

"One PP is coming down hard on both of these cases. Everts, can you shed some insight here?" Zeile cuts in, his voice strained.

"I didn't get to do much digging, but I think Keets was suffering from PTSD," Will says. "He would have had an interesting case of mental disease or defect."

"So, in essence, a soldier who needed help died in your care? Why wasn't he in a mental facility instead of jail awaiting arraignment?" Carter's voice rises.

Zeile shouts back, "Because Keets refused to speak to our psychologists, let alone wait months for an appointment at the VA. His cousin has power of attorney and didn't want him forcibly medicated either. Then there's the little fact that he was being held on multiple murder charges. Where the hell did you think he would go? My officers followed protocol! We're in the business of following the law, not reading minds or making decisions for people. We reopened the case when more information came to light. We will continue to proceed with the investigation—"

"No, you won't. The Pentagon will be handling it henceforth." Carter moves away from his team and heads for the door. "Sergeant Everts, you will be handing everything over to us immediately."

"I understand the request, Major General, but—"

"Do as he says, Everts," Zeile says. "Is that all you came here to do? This could have been handled over the phone." He's right, there was no reason to come here and demand control. A simple phone call would have been sufficient.

"The Pentagon wanted to inform you that our investigation will also involve this precinct and your team, Captain Zeile. If there was any impropriety, we will find it. Good day," Major General Carter says before walking out the door. Will looks back at the rest of us, then reluctantly follows Carter and closes the door behind him.

"Okay then, back to Schlect," Zeile says. "Someone please give me something."

"We have five hours before we're required to charge or release him," Logan mutters.

"Something helpful," Zeile says. He unlocks his phone and flops into a chair.

"Media attention got kicked into high gear from the *New York Times*," Logan says. "Apparently he sent them a package to be opened at noon today. It ran online before hitting the evening edition." He spins his laptop around and shows everyone at the table.

Frankie reaches for the computer. "May I?" Logan pushes it in her direction.

"After the *Times* published the op-ed, TMZ grabbed it, followed by social media and other news outlets," Logan finishes.

"Which means all the families know," Sydney adds.

"If he admits guilt in the article, we've got him," Logan says.

"I thought you were the scientist," Sydney says. "Where's the evidence? What's to say this isn't just a hoax?"

"Maybe he's got something from one of the crime scenes," Logan says.

"He's too smart for that. Why would he come here and play us but then just release what is basically a confession to the press? It doesn't fit," I add.

"He didn't." The entire room focuses on Frankie, who keeps her eyes glued to Logan's computer screen. "His word choices, phraseology . . . it's almost perfect. Schlect continues to make inferences to his deeds but never actually admits to the act itself. He only talks about things the police have already released and he never once connects himself to the victims." She looks up from the computer. "He's playing the long game here, and he fully expects to win."

"Coming in here was the first move," Sydney says softly.

"Exactly. He put you in a position, expecting the desired result," Frankie says.

"I went to the bar and spoke to the school. Found his connections, but nothing of substance," I say.

"Which is exactly what you should have done. It was procedure, and you might think you've moved forward in the game, but . . ."

"It's part of the bigger strategy to kick my ass. We're playing his game and his rules, not ours."

"Precisely. You need to figure out his next move and counter it. It might not be legal or even ethical. You have to think like him, Jasmine."

"Easier said than done, Dr. Ryan," Zeile says. "We've got nothing but his words, some minor evidence that leads us nowhere, and an article that was written by his own hand. I'm not feeling very confident at the moment." He leans back in his chair.

"Let me go back in there and talk with him," I say. The room falls into an uncomfortable silence. "He wanted to talk to me in the first place. Let me show him that I took the bait and he won the round. Maybe he tells me something, maybe not. You guys keep crunching the numbers and profile. Let me talk to the piece of shit."

Captain Zeile stands and puts his suit jacket back on. "Okay, but the first indication of this going sideways and Doctor Ryan pulls you out of there. In the meantime, Locke, work on a statement with legal. Discuss with them how to handle the victims' families before calling all of them. Make sure you follow their advice explicitly. We don't need to incite a riot. After that, I'll make a statement to the press while the rest of you work your asses off to figure out how we keep him here. I don't care if it's a parking ticket from Montana ten years ago. Find me something. The entire precinct is at your disposal. Use the manpower."

Zeile and Locke quickly head out of the room to their respective tasks. Logan grabs his computer, flips it closed, and drops his cell into his back pocket. "I'll work better with my full system and staff in the dungeon. I'll call if I find anything," he says and walks out of the room.

"You sure you can handle this?" Frankie asks.

"Is anyone ever prepared for something like this?" My hands ball into fists as I try to mentally prepare for the interview.

"You said you went back to the bar."

"I had to," I say. I know where she's steering this conversation, and I'm trying like hell to avoid it.

"Jasmine, if you need to talk about it . . ."

"Frankie, I love you with every ounce of my being, but I can't focus on that right now. This isn't the time for it." I sound harsher than I intend.

"I didn't mean now. When this is finished, you need to talk to me. You promised no more shutting down. Give me your word," she says and crosses her arms tightly across her chest.

"You have my word." I kiss her forehead, looking for some comfort. Leaning back, I feel the mask come down over my face, the cold harshness of my other persona. The one who hides, locks away all emotion, and goes after people like Schlect.

***

The room is slightly colder than before, both in temperature and in tension. A paper cup full of coffee, probably cold, rests in the center of the table. Schlect stands in front of the one-way mirror eerily staring at himself, his hands clasped behind him and his back rigidly straight.

As I walk farther into the room, he spins on his heels and, in one fluid motion, sits in the chair closest to the mirror, effectively putting himself in the interviewer's position—the position of power. His back effectively blocks Frankie from seeing any subtle expression or twitch of his face. The cameras angled at the other chair will be blind to his musings.

There's always a power struggle with psychopathic personalities, especially someone who feels they are always one step ahead. The question for me is how to proceed. We're in a police station, but I'm not sure I feel entirely comfortable alone in the room with him, especially with him unrestrained. There's an unpredictability that I have to account for. The interviewer's chair is closer to the door and a safe exit. Me sitting in the other chair gives him an advantage both mentally and strategically.

He looks over to me and waves to the chair across the table. I nod before I step out and motion to the officer nearest the pen. His name tag reads Hucek. He's a familiar face from a shift I'm not familiar with: the late shift. Our paths have only crossed occasionally.

"Officer Hucek, who uncuffed him?"

He's a big, swarthy man in his thirties and obviously has a few years under his belt. Enough for me to know he wouldn't have done this on his own. "Captain requested it. I think it's cause he's not been charged with nothing yet."

I stare and make a decision. "I'd like you in the room with me then, please."

"No problem, detective."

I step back into the room and Karl looks up. Then he notices Hucek behind me.

"Tsk-tsk, Jasmine. You don't feel at ease alone with me in this room?"

I ignore the comment and stand at the wall opposite him. "Karl . . ."

"Jasmine. You were doing such a good job building rapport, and now this." He nods his head toward Hucek, who stands against the wall near the door. I lean over and look into the paper cup. "Maybe you're not as worthy as I thought."

"Didn't like your coffee?" I ask, making sure I'm leaning over him so he has to look up to me to speak. I saunter back to the wall.

"It was nothing to write home about."

"There's a Starbucks down the street. I'm sure we could get you something more palatable to your tastes."

"I prefer to brew my own Italian espresso roast at home. I'll have a cup soon, but thank you for the offer," he says, looking at his watch. "I'm guessing you checked in with Xavier?"

"He speaks highly of you. Says the students enjoy your classes. Apparently, you're a model teacher there." I embellish everything to stoke his ego. I shift away from the wall and make a point of standing behind him while I speak. "Then again, Clinical Interviewing could be taught by any fool with a psychology degree. You just have to read from the book and use the standard tests. Lord knows my professor did. Even the basic psych classes you handled can't be that involved. It's not like you're instilling the value of profiling, addictions, or forensic analysis of a crime scene into the future generations of America. You just want to make them understand how to talk to people in a specific situation. *Sesame Street* offers more information."

"The younger generations are ill-equipped to speak, let alone communicate," he says. "They live in a world of shitty emojis and text language. The young ladies are the most ill-equipped to deal with anything presented to them outside of likes or followers. Without me, civil communication would cease to exist."

"Maybe, but in the bigger picture of John Jay College, you are primarily an undergraduate professor who gets kids through required classes. You do the same at the graduate level when they throw you a class every now and then. You don't rock the boat, but you don't build it either. You just exist to row and move it along." I stop, bend over the table, and rest my fists on it, knuckles down. My hands turn white from the pressure. "You're a cog in the bigger machine. You disappear into the crowd because you're nothing."

"Maybe the crowd is where I want to stay. It's quiet, calm, and attracts less attention," he counters. "I enjoy diversifying my talents, giving a little bit to anyone willing to accept the attention. You, Detective Jasmine Steele, are a one-trick pony with systematic answers, by-the-book decisions, and a love of your own worth. The way you went after Garrison was nothing short of pure egomaniacal behavior. You add nothing to this scenario; you only detract from it." His eyes squint ever so slightly. "You are a villain in your own story."

"Possibly . . . Maybe I am a narcissistic fool, but I'm the one who had people standing in the back to hear me speak. I have name recognition in my alma mater, my city, and with the FBI." I pull the chair out and sit down, resting my feet on the table, making sure the bottom of my shoes face him—an insult in some countries. "Let's cut through the crap. You're wasting my time. Either you have something to offer this investigation or you get the hell out of my precinct," I say. He doesn't flinch. "I am curious though. Did you invest in the bar to get women more pliable to your whims or was it a business endeavor?"

"Is that what you've deduced, detective?"

Silence falls over the room for several minutes. His face remains still, revealing nothing. I snake my arms slowly around my midsection. My eyes never leave his. My heels remain firmly planted on the table. In a game such as this, there's one simple rule: do not break contact unless you have the next move planned out.

"You're trying to test me, but all you are doing is wasting time."

He obviously knows what move to bring this game to the next level.

"Maybe I am, but I still own you until we either arrest you for serving minors or a parking ticket for all I care. I've got time," I say and stand up. He casually glances at his watch.

"Do you though? Looks like you've only got about another twenty minutes left on your side." He leans forward and sighs. "Time is such a fickle thing. As children, it's this entity we cannot understand and yet we chase it. We're taught that with age comes knowledge, respect, and opportunities for new things. Then we are left to drift in the waters of time, slowly drowning in the speed with which life is passing us all by. So, I ask again, do you really believe you have all the time in the world? Or that our killer's next victims do?"

"Not all the time in the world. I only said that I have these few fleeting moments to engage with you before something comes up that will alleviate this crunch and allow us to continue our pursuit of you in regard to the murders of these four women. You should relish these minutes right now. The ones where your wrists aren't shackled to your ankles. Where the air conditioning and two-way mirror offer you entertainment. In the near future, you'll be sitting in a cell with no windows. Your every thought, plate of food, what you read, and your masturbatory habits will be monitored." I shrug.

"You really think so, detective?" He laughs. "Why, you haven't even charged me with a crime. What makes you think—"

"You're going away, Schlect. You're not nearly as smart as you think. Everything ends today."

He begins to slowly clap his hands. "Bravo, bravo! I bring out the best in you, Jasmine." He leans forward, his chest pressing against the metal. "But you're so self-absorbed, detective. It wasn't our short time together that I was lamenting."

The acid in my stomach churns at his words. The game has another player. One we're not aware of. My gaze shifts, solely focused on his next words.

"Humor me, Jasmine. Do you remember the first car accident you were ever in?"

"Of course."

"The first arrest you ever made?"

"Yes."

"The first time you ever shot another human being?"

"Yes," I say. "Is there a point to this?"

"We never forget the first time we do something dramatic in our lives. It's ingrained in the recesses of our minds, fully accessible at any given moment." He stands, looks at his watch, and straightens his shirt.

"But those are all in the past," I say.

The door opens and Zeile stands there, a look of resignation on his face. That's when I know we have nothing to hold him.

"Ticktock, ticktock, Detective Steele." He glances one last time at his watch. "I must be going, but it was lovely . . . talking with you," he says and holds out his hand. Against my better judgment, I clasp his hand. He pulls me full force to him, his free arm around my back in a hug. Officer Hucek lurches toward us, but I hold up a hand to stop him.

Schlect whispers in my ear, "Why would you forget the one that started it all? Why remove her from the world when you can keep her and relive the glory all over again? Her life's always in my hands. She's desperate for the sustenance that I give on a weekly visit. Her screams entice me more than any other woman I've had. Making her mine over and over again—it's glorious and fills in the gaps between dance partners."

My hand clenches his tighter. He lets go and shakes my hand free before walking out of the room. From down the hall I can hear him say, "Ticktock, ticktock."

"Please tell me you heard him," I say.

"No, what did he say?"

"If you didn't hear it, neither did the cameras." I walk right up to Zeile. "He admitted his first victim is still alive to be assaulted whenever he desires. We need to find something to bring him in before he's in the wind."

Gunfire pulls everyone back to the present. Three quick shots. I flatten myself against the wall, while Hucek pulls his service revolver and quickly checks the hall. Screams echo off the concrete. I open the conference room and see Frankie hiding under the table, safe. She moves toward me, but my hand stops her. I mouth "stay" and close the door before she can argue.

Officers rush past us down the hallway, obscuring the initial view of the scene. I follow the crowd out the front door and into the street. White flashbulbs go off in rapid succession. Zeile stands with one hand on his hip and the other in his hair, screaming something to an officer next to him.

The sounds of the crowd fade away as an ever-growing dark pool of blood forms on the sidewalk. Karl Schlect lies on his back, eyes staring at the darkened sky, his shirt with three small red marks. Several officers try to prevent the media from getting proper images, but there's no hiding the scene.

Two other officers push an older, white-haired male through the throng and up the stairs into the precinct. I can only assume he's the one who shot Schlect. Another officer follows behind, holding a small-caliber handgun hanging on his pencil so as not to disturb any prints.

Dread washes over me as I watch the blood continue to flow out of Schlect. I lost the battle, but he enticed me into another round with information of his first victim. He's kept her alive for this long, and I assume she's well hidden from the world. He must give her food, water, and other sustenance. This means someone out there definitely doesn't have all the time in the world.

Chapter Eleven

The morgue is always the quietest place in the entire building. That's especially true today. The media frenzy outside has increased exponentially with the murder of Karl Schlect. Once every channel and social media feed was filled with video of the shooting, the captain moved the press back to a full one-block perimeter. His press conference conveyed the available details while explaining it was an ongoing investigation.

Schlect walked into our precinct, annoyed at the original newspaper article, and was shot after his own *Times* op-ed implied he was the killer. They say serial killers are meticulous and rarely caught if they manage to keep their composure. BTK, Ted Bundy—they were caught due to mistakes brought on by ego. One wanted the press and notoriety of being a serial killer. He was long gone and forgotten until he contacted the local papers. The other thought he was smarter but couldn't control his compulsion and killed without his normal plan. They both needed control and were caught because of their lapse in judgment.

Karl Schlect belongs right there with the two of those men. He probably wanted to put more pressure on our team to put his name back in the headlines. He never anticipated the readers wouldn't follow the article with the same intrigue like the Zodiac's letters. They would follow the conclusions of the media and online communities. He was dead the minute the first person pointed the finger at him on Twitter.

No one in the precinct went home after the shooting. Some members of the press were too close to the crime, and their clothing and equipment sit with Dr. Brown in forensics. They're now waiting to give their statements to uniformed officers for the DA.

The rest of us remain, sleeping in shifts in the locker rooms. Once awake, we were dragged into an interview room with Internal Affairs, their questioning conducted in quick-fire sessions, hoping you slip up or give them a set of answers to cover the entire NYPD from a lawsuit. In this situation, they're as helpful as an enema for a broken arm. Yet here I sit, in the quiet of the morgue, watching Schlect's liver being weighed. No closer to closing this case than before he walked into my interview room.

Victor moves slowly and mechanically through the procedure. Most of the time, it's a rather disgusting practice to witness. The body is photographed thoroughly. Evidence is collected from the external areas and orifices, then washed clean, and then a scalpel splits the flesh open. Body parts are checked, removed, and placed in the metal scale. Dictation is recorded for a future report that may never see the light of day or help us in this case.

He does all this meticulous work to give a voice to those who can no longer speak. Those words hit my ears so often that it feels like a cliché. Yet, here he is, talking to the victim as he tries to understand what happened. The rational side of me thinks that's a waste of time considering the man is no longer breathing. The psychological part of my brain reminds me that we're both surrounded by death every day. Sometimes we need a few unconventional means to deal with it. Otherwise, we'd all be alcoholics, drug addicts, or villains ourselves.

Watching his routine calms the burning discontent slowly growing in my stomach. The last words of a killer remain at the forefront of my mind. There's one more victim out there, and we might be able to save her.

"How long can someone survive without food or water?" I ask.

"Depends on a lot of things. Gandhi survived twenty-one days of total starvation with only sips of water. A body can go a long time without food, but that could also depend on your genetics, current BMI, and a ton of other factors. Overall the scientific consensus is about three weeks give or take without food. Water is a different story; you'll have around three days." Victor pauses and looks over at me. "Going on an extreme diet? There are some horrific side effects beyond the obvious risk of death."

"Three weeks . . ." My mind wanders off.

"Three weeks no food. Again, you'd die long before that without any fluids in your system." He pulls out the long intestine and coils it into the scale. "You seem to be missing that part."

"Explain."

"Jasmine, it's basic biology. We're mostly made of water. It's in our blood and joints, it flushes out waste, and it assists in temperature control. Of course, outside temperatures, health, and a lot of other factors can change the duration by a day or so. Three to four days is about the max," he finishes. "Why?"

"Schlect told me he kept his first victim alive for encore performances," I say. "Tell Lillian I need her to get on those samples you sent her ASAP. If you find anything abnormal, shoot me a message. I'll be upstairs trying to convince the powers that be we might have a chance at redemption."

★★★

Voices echo down the hallway and only increase in intensity as I get closer to the conference room. I know from the tone the captain is getting reamed.

I knock on the door and hear the voices hush as I wait. "Come in," a deep voice, unknown to me, says. Walking into the room, I see Zeile sitting in his usual seat at the head of the table, beneath the one window in the room. To his left and right are several suits—lawyers or power people—all sitting rigidly in their chairs. Will and Sydney sit at the other end, looking small and unassuming in their chairs. The tension punches me square in the face, making every step into the room difficult.

"Steele, what do you need?" Zeile asks.

"Cap, I think we need to discuss the last words of Schlect before—"

A man directly to the left of Zeile interrupts me. "He was murdered in front of your precinct. Two deaths in twenty-four hours must be a record!" It's the same powerful voice that ordered my entry.

"Technically Keets died on Rikers awaiting trial, not in holding here," I say. "Schlect was murdered out of our custody. We had to let him go. But don't let facts get in the way of your diatribe."

"Watch it, detective," he says.

"I would, but time is of the essence and you're wasting mine."

"One more word and I'll have your badge!"

"Why don't we all calm down here!" Zeile stands quickly, drawing all attention to him. "Everts, has Major General Carter taken all the information on Keets from the precinct?"

"Yes, sir. At this point, they are in the lead and will call if they need assistance," Will says. "Commissioner, I understand you are disturbed by the two situations, but Steele is correct. Neither individual was in our custody at the time of either incident. While protocols can be increased to give more security, we can only plan for so many extraneous variables."

"Commissioner?" I mouth to Will. He nods his head slowly.

"That's a great speech, Everts. Want to give that to the general public? I'm sure they would love to hear it isn't our fault. That doesn't work," Zeile says.

"It would if you kept the rogue assholes with a badge under wraps, but the wall of blue—"

"Sydney!" Will cuts her off before any damage can be done to her career.

The commissioner abruptly stands, smooths the bottom of his suit jacket, and nods to the rest of his entourage. Two of them pile stacks of files into their briefcases and file out of the room. The rest follow silently, leaving their boss alone.

"I'll say this once and only once. This precinct and all parties involved with these two cases will be under increased scrutiny. We will be considering any and all measures to ensure the negative press does not damage the reputation of the entire NYPD. I understand you are new here, Captain Zeile, but maybe this position is not a good fit for you."

He walks to the door and stops right next to me. "You were given a break for the Garrison case due to the positive press it received. You won't be receiving the same treatment this time around." He leaves, slamming the door so hard it bounces back halfway.

"He's pleasant," Frankie says as she walks through the open doorway.

"Dr. Ryan, thank you for coming back on such short notice," Zeile says. He settles back into his chair.

"Of course." She squeezes my hand and looks me in the eyes. "Did you get any sleep?"

I shrug my shoulders. "I'll be fine. How's Chase?"

"Playing video games and wondering when you're planning on helping him get past the zombie boss from hell."

The words warm my heart, and I would love to kiss her right now. Keeping our professional distance, I smile while holding her hand as tightly as I can. Frankie turns away from our intimate moment and takes a seat next to the captain.

"So, what did you find?" he asks.

"Not much. Several evaluations were done over the years. They all indicate that Schlect was diagnosed with narcissistic personality disorder in his teenage years. Every report felt he had psychopathic tendencies. The first one was completed when he was only sixteen and concluded if his psychosis was not addressed, it would escalate."

"How did he fall through the cracks? With these reports, someone could have done something," Sydney says.

"Doesn't matter right now, Locke. Doctor Ryan, did these papers give you any other information we can use?"

"Firstly, he never fell through the cracks. These kinds of records can be sealed since he never committed a crime and was a minor. I wish I had more for you, but I don't. The judge gave us emergency access, but we don't know if he was sent to different doctors, ever used an alias . . . We're at a dead end," Frankie concludes.

"Who shot Schlect?" I ask.

"General Henry Smith," Sydney says quietly.

"Smith? Emelia's father?" I quickly toss out.

"The very one," Zeile says. "Locke contacted every family and gave them each the official statement. It took time, and unfortunately General Smith was already moving forward with his final mission."

Those words are so very true; it would be his last free moment. Being a military man, Smith knew the act of shooting anyone would give him a sentence equivalent to death. The minute Schlect's body stopped breathing, he would be given twenty years or more. Considering his age, he'll die upstate somewhere. The conditions surrounding his actions might bring him some sympathy, and I have a feeling the Pentagon will want his case. He's a decorated war hero with national security clearance. Carter will want to hide him to keep those secrets hidden.

"Carter had to give him a heads-up," Will mutters to our surprise. "I'm just saying what you're all thinking."

"No matter what we believe, we won't be throwing around accusations. That's not how we operate," Zeile says. "We might be up shit creek here, but we may have another victim if we don't focus our attention."

"Shouldn't you have led with that?" Sydney says, sitting up a little straighter in her chair.

"We were getting to it. Dr. Ryan was going over the medical history of our perpetrator," Zeile finishes. "Steele, why do you look like you're going to throw up?"

"Because our timeline just shrunk exponentially while I was talking to Victor." I grab a piece of paper and a pen. "Schlect told me he was planning on visiting his living victim the next day. He mentioned going to her once a week. He said she would be desperate for sustenance by the time he gets to her." I scribble some numbers on the piece of paper, basic math that my brain can't seem to compute at the moment. "We have anywhere from a minimum of twelve hours to a maximum of forty-eight hours to find her. It's just a guess, but much longer than that and we are in code red territory."

"I understand this needs to be of the utmost importance, but we cannot deny the other side of the equation here," Frankie says. "This woman might not exist. This might be another game. We could be using taxpayer resources for nothing. We just need to be prepared for that possible outcome and the retribution that might follow from your superiors."

"I agree with Dr. Ryan, and I understand we can't afford another misstep right now," Zeile says. "We'll assume your numbers are right for the girl. I don't want to play games with this. Until further notice, everyone is working."

"I need a warrant for Dreamers Den, his adjunct office at John Jay, and whatever apartment he has listed," I say.

"Everts will take the school. You go to his apartment. Locke will handle the bar. I want Mr. Levy and Dr. Brown kept in the loop with all information. Forensics might not be what solves cases, but it's the nail in the fucking coffin. So, let's go."

"Sir . . ."

"That's my decision, and it's final. Divide and conquer." Zeile stands and leaves the conference room, followed by Will and Sydney.

Frankie hangs back and closes the door behind them. Her hands grip my arms tightly as her eyes scan mine. "Sweetheart, you need to talk to me."

"Now is most assuredly not the time."

"It will take a few minutes for Captain Zeile to call the DA or ADA and get a judge to sign off. We're in a holding pattern until then."

"I could be waiting outside of the apartment for the call to come in."

There are moments in life that we have to face daily, but right now, I don't want to. I want my attention on the woman who could be dying somewhere waiting for her keeper to come home. My mind is focused on rushing out the door and ransacking everything and anything, regardless of rules or regulations. If not for the massive bull's-eye we seem to have acquired on our doors, I would be doing just that.

Frankie sits in a chair, patiently waiting.

"I saw him at that bar when I was going to grad school; you know this," I say. "Why do you need me to repeat myself?"

"Because you've never really talked about it at all. In fact, you just mentioned you never wanted to hang out there ever again." Frankie grabs my hand, rubs her thumb over my skin, and kisses my palm. "I know whatever happened is difficult for you. I also know we promised to put secrets behind us. Going back to the bar churned up something negative, and it's my job as your fiancée to help you handle it before you let that energy overwhelm you."

"Doesn't help to have your family in town, having to deal with their judgment and the possibility of another body on our heads. Just a great day, dear!" I snap. My phone vibrates, taking both of our attention away from the matter. Logan's sent me a message with Schlect's address in Washington Heights. "I love you, but I can't do this right now—I don't have the time—and I need you to respect that."

She drops my hand, stands up, and opens the door. "I'm going to go into your office if anyone needs me. Until then, I want you to remember that my family might be as messed up as ever, but they're part of me. They're my blood, for better or worse. They're also kind enough to watch our son while we're working on this case. In fact, my father commended you on your dedication to this case. He might not have said it in the way I would like, but it was a step in the right direction. My point is all this negative blame game bullshit doesn't work with me anymore. So, I'd appreciate it if you could move beyond it," Frankie says as she leaves the conference room.

Normally I would have felt guilty for not answering her questions, but right now, I don't. My mind can't access the darkest trenches of my childhood without having a drink. Not to mention the need to get back to the surface and focus on the task I have to find this missing woman. I don't know how I'm going to tell Frankie everything, but when this is handled, hopefully I'll be able to.

I shoot a text back to Logan asking him to look deeper at Shawn Brandy. His financials might be an open book, but maybe he has an inter-net presence we aren't aware of. I want him to rip everything apart, from the schools he attended to when he lost his virginity. No holds barred, no kindness, no bullshit. The response is immediate: a thumbs-up emoji. Right now, the best place I can be is parked in front of the apartment building, waiting for someone to contact me.

My phone rings as I walk out of the conference room. "Steele."

"Detective, the warrant is signed and in my hand. Go," the captain tells me quickly before hanging up.

Pushing through the crowd to my car, I duck under the police tape which is still out front. The mass of people outside waiting for another press release push against the cruiser as I pass the barricades, all of them moving about as if this was the most important part of their day. None of them know something darker is looming around the corner.

A woman, locked in a box or a small room—no water, no food, screaming for help, and no one can hear her. Those people can't comprehend that. It's not in their wheelhouse. I wish it were never part of mine.

Even if we find her in time, if she is in fact real, there will always be someone screaming. Sometimes, it's me.

The size of Schlect's first-floor apartment is rather impressive. The old building has a small courtyard for all three units on this floor. After fighting with the manager for a few minutes and showing him a copy of the warrant on my phone, he opened the door and quickly left. I'm sure he doesn't want anything to do with us in his building.

The forensic team is on its way, so I am careful not to disturb specific items. Using latex gloves, I push the door open into an open dining room, kitchen, living room combination. One door off the kitchen leads to the outdoor space. The three others must lead to the two bedrooms and a bathroom.

Closing the door behind me, I head into the kitchen. One cabinet is slightly ajar, revealing two boxes of unopened breakfast cereal. The adjacent door houses canned goods from vegetables to soups. Nothing of interest near or around them. The next set of cabinets hold glassware, plates, and coffee mugs. Everything is meticulously stacked in a precise, orderly fashion.

The fridge is the same. Plastic containers with labels on them labeled for each day. Each day a clean, organized pile of three green, red, and clear bins. The writing on top indicates red is for meat, green for vegetables, and clear for a carbohydrate or fruit. Water bottles fill the entire bottom row of the narrow unit. Everything points to the reports showing Schlect's need and desire to control every aspect of life. It must have given him some sense of calm to just grab what was needed and not have to think about it.

A small dining room table hugs the wall. Two wooden chairs sit at each end. Both sides could be raised to increase the surface area. There are no other chairs anywhere. Classic loner behavior.

The living room takes up the majority of the apartment. A black leather couch shimmers, looking almost wet. I run my hand across the surface. It feels and smells like it's recently been cleaned and possibly lotioned as well. A blanket, neatly folded, rests along the back. The couch recliner buttons smell of a bleach-based cleaning agent.

The glass entertainment center holds no dust or fingerprints that my eye can detect. The television, towers holding movies, and video games appear wiped clean as well. It is obvious the entire main area has been scrubbed down to ensure there isn't a speck of evidence left behind. Schlect expected us to be here relatively soon after his interview. He ensured there would be no evidence left behind to collect. It was a smart move if he had made it home alive.

The first door on my right leads to a barren excuse for a bedroom. The sparse furniture includes a desk, a two-drawer wood file cabinet, and an old office chair. The wood floor is bare. The sole trash can is empty. There's a shredder next to the desk. Lifting up the top with the edge of my jacket sleeve, I see my suspicions were correct. It's empty—another dead end.

The second door leads to a more realistic-sized bedroom. The double pressure doors open up to a simple closet. The left side has shelving from floor to ceiling. Each level has a different item of clothing or linens. Everything is folded perfectly and organized with purpose. Shoes are lined up on the floor: tall boots in the back row, the front row split between sneakers and dressier ones. Picking up a pair in the front, I see the treads are clean. I grab one from the back; the same thing rings true. No evidence.

Pants are hung perfectly on the clothes rack, organized by color, jeans then dress slacks. Shirts, both those hanging in the closet and the ones in the dresser, are pristine and orderly. Nothing in this entire apartment so far can assist me in getting one step closer to the mind of this maniac. He's got control issues, but that doesn't help me one fucking bit. The queen size bed that I know for a fact he would never bring a victim to sits untouched.

"Detective?" a voice from the forensic team calls out.

"One minute."

Walking into the living room, I see several forensic team members in full hazmat getup waiting for my go-ahead. Hopefully they can find something before I lose my mind in this meticulous madness.

"Rip this place apart. Find me something, anything."

The six techs flood the place, each heading into a different room. The captain promised no expense would be spared just in case there is another victim. Nothing puts my mind at ease right now. There are no personal photos anywhere I can see. No paintings or posters. Nothing to give this place an individualistic touch. This is strictly home base for a psycho in between his hunting activities.

I step into the courtyard to get a breath. The cool breeze forces hairs to stand at attention as I look around. No table outside, just a beautiful stone patio and a homemade greenhouse. Elaborate electric components run along one side, leading to a covered outdoor outlet. That must be some kind of temperature control for the cold winters. A small lock holds it all closed. I tap on the glass and point a tech to the door.

"I need bolt cutters," I say, the cold making my voice waver and my teeth chatter.

The tech hands me a massive pair of cutters that could easily lop off a human finger. I look down at the luggage-sized master lock and have to laugh. This is the epitome of overkill. Angling the lock between the blade, I squeeze the handles and easily snap both sides. The slightly bleached black lock falls to the ground. I toss the cutters back to the tech, slip the latch open, and step inside.

You can clean up every drop of dust or dirt. You can remove everything you think might be found to implicate yourself. Yet there's a human tendency to overlook the things we love or admire. I could never remove my computer or clean it to the point of being useless to investigators. Schlect couldn't remove this greenhouse filled with his children. It would be like throwing away his favorite murder weapon. The beautifully blooming white carnations cover the shelves. The bottom rows house smaller pots with what appears to be fresh new growth. Below the last shelf is a small set of gardening gloves and a cutter.

"I need this all bagged. Soil, pots . . . I want it all," I say to the tech standing next to me.

Pulling out my phone, I dial Zeile.

"Steele, find anything?"

"A greenhouse with white carnations. Doesn't help find the girl, but it looks like we might have evidence proving he's the Carnation Killer. Beyond that, the place is absolutely spotless. I'll have to wait on the science techs to do their thing," I say. "Any luck from the other locations?"

"The office was shared space, so nothing useful. We have tons of papers from the bar. Locke and Everts are flipping through it quickly, looking for anything, but forensics will continue to go through it all piece by piece."

"I'll come back and lend a hand. This place looks like it's staged to sell. I doubt they'll find anything beyond the obvious, but you never know."

"We're burning our time faster than I'd like. Emergency police protocol," Zeile replies.

The phone disconnects and the gravity of the situation continues to push me further into darkness. Zeile just told me to go against the books and use my sirens. I've done it before, but being given permission just makes this situation feel all the more dire.

Chapter Twelve

The conference room is crowded once again but this time with boxes instead of people. Sydney is at the head of the table, an empty box at her feet and a stack of paper in front of her. She grabs a sheet, scans it quickly, and either puts it in front of her or back into the box. Every few seconds she runs her hand along her neck and attempts to stretch. Between the Keets case and this, Sydney has gotten a trial by fire. I feel bad for her, but in the end, it will make her a stronger detective.

Will stands at the far side of the table, boxes all around him. He scans pages, sorts through a box quickly, and then drops it back to the floor. I don't understand what his process is, but it doesn't look very effective. His muscles strain against his shirt as he lifts another box onto the table and flips the top off. I wonder how his gunshot wound feels with all his exertion.

I hang my jacket on the back of the chair in front of me and grab a box from the floor. Flipping it open, I see there are several file folders with random scribbling on the headers. The papers within are old tax forms, discolored with age. I doubt they were on the up-and-up with the government, so this box will have to go to Forensic Accounting. The rest of the box seems like more of the same. I close it and place it away from the others. I don't want to waste time going through the same one twice.

The next box appears to be random loose papers. Some receipts from liquor companies. Payroll information. Another box for the people with windows in their offices. The next two are more of the same. Lots of normal, random items that seem to fill the needs of running a bar.

"Found some photos," Sydney pipes up. "Several women in the bar with Brandy."

"Look like patrons? Adults? Gotta give me more than that, Sydney," Will says.

"These girls are not legal by any stretch. I'd bet my yearly salary on it," she says. She slides a stack of photos to Will.

His eyes scan each one quickly as his face turns redder.

"Add it to the 'illegal activity involving minors' section." He hands her back the photos.

Sydney closes the box and walks it to the corner where there are already six stacked high. She looks at the pile and starts a new one adjacent to it.

"So, I'm going on the assumption Dreamers Den was a pedophile's playground?" I ask.

"From what I've seen thus far, it was more of a place for the owner to get his rocks off. Doesn't seem like any of his clients were getting their kicks, though I wouldn't put it past them," Will says. He grabs another box and begins to look through it, slower this time.

I grab the one near my feet and flip the top onto the table. Some random photos of women, smiling. Another of an elderly woman hugging her two dogs. An older woman cooking in the kitchen for what I can only assume was a party based on the number of pots on the stove. The images show what looks like a normal American family.

The papers under the photos are faded and impossible to read. Forensics might be able to see what is written with their light instruments, so I put them to the side. Another receipt grabs my attention: Flowers by Janine, Garden City. The handwritten receipt logged some carnation bulbs, several bags of potting soil, and on the bottom lists two bags of *Age-Old Bloom*. They paid in cash.

"Captain," I yell. "I think I found something."

Zeile rushes in, his tie long gone and his top button undone. His hair is a mess, and he looks ragged, like we all do right now.

"What is it?"

I say nothing and hand him the receipt. I know he's read the file and knows all the pertinent information in it. No need to say it again.

"Brandy?" he asks.

"Paid cash. Might not have been just Schlect. It could have been Brandy. Or both of them," I answer.

"Which makes the DA's case against General Smith even stronger." He hands the pages back to me. "What are these behind you? You sort through them?"

"Forensic Accounting; it's all the taxes and other crap like it."

"What about that one by you, Locke?" He points to the leaning tower of boxes.

"All kiddie porn, underage liquor sales, you name it."

"Okay, I can start moving them out of here then. I'll get accounting down here and have SVU pick up the rest." He grabs the box behind me and moves out of the room.

The only other captain I've ever had who was in the trenches with us was Tyler Udall. When he died, I never thought we'd have another good one. Hell, I never thought this Yankees fan would hold his weight, let alone fill those shoes. Today, he's earning my respect.

I place the incriminating receipt over to the side, where I start a pile of what will hopefully be Carnation Killer evidence. The next few pages are so worn from being folded into a square, they almost rip apart as I open them. My gloved hands tentatively pull the pages apart on the table. The grooves look like worn leather creases, the edges yellowed from oxygen and poor packing. The words are almost completely gone, but the faded header remains: Garden City High School.

Another folder behind it holds meaningless papers, notes, and other ramblings that a psychologist will have to evaluate. I continue to dig and come across a few more photos. Two young teens kneeling, each with one hand on their football helmets, in full uniform. I remember seeing a similar photo behind the bar of Dreamers Den.

I toss the photos on the pile of new information and delve deeper into the box. A small square, the size of a credit card, slides under my thumbnail in the glove, causing a hole. A blood spot appears under the glove. I move my hand away to prevent any contamination of the evidence. Using my other hand, I pull the offending object out. The cheap plastic frame holds a photo of the same two boys, but older, with their arms around a beautiful young woman, all wearing what appear to be graduation gowns. The boy on the right still has his cap on; the other two are missing theirs. On the back it says CUNY Graduation Day.

Flipping through several other images, the same female shows up in all of them. It's hard to tell if the rest were taken before or after graduation, but there is always one of the boys in each image with her.

My cell phone beeps. I check the screen. It's Logan asking if we've found anything.

"Guys, I'm going to take these photos down to Logan and see if he can do some facial recognition. I also found some high school and college documentation, so if you catch anything like that, put it to the side, okay?"

"On it," Sydney agrees, and Will nods as he digs into another box.

I snap off the torn glove, toss it in the trash, and grab a new one. If these images are younger versions of Brandy and Schlect, maybe it will lead somewhere.

***

I grab the small handful of photos and head to the elevator. The usual ding announcing my arrival on the tech floor seems to take longer than usual. There are more people down in the pits of the precinct than before. Eyeballing a path through the techs, I can hear Logan talking over most of them. Holding my hand above the heads, I point toward the large corner office. Logan nods his head and starts heading to meet me.

Walking into the office, I step around Logan's desk and carefully put down the few things I pulled out of the box upstairs.

"I don't know if these give us anything, but if Brandy and Schlect go back all the way to high school, then maybe there's something we didn't think of."

"Could be. That was before the internet and social media, so this might take some time. But let's start with a simple search of the high school and college." Logan types frantically. "I have a random question for you."

"If you can ask while you're working, go for it," I answer and stare at the screen behind his desk.

"Has Hadley spoken to you recently?"

"No, last I saw her was at that awards dinner."

"She's in LA right now. Some minor reshoots. Then a marketing tour for a few months before she comes back home. I might go to see her when she's in London. Do the whole touristy thing—Jack the Ripper tour and all that stuff."

"Sounds like she's fine. Focus, Logan. Are you finding anything?"

"Not yet."

"I told her if she ever needed me to just text or call. I don't want to bother her while she's living out her dream. Maybe I'm a bad friend, but a text saying 'hi' is more than enough for me."

"It's not that . . ."

The search stops with two names blinking in highlighted yellow.

"Schlect and Brandy have known each other since 2002 as freshmen when they were on the JV football team," Logan says as he clicks a few other keys. The two names come up again when CUNY Queens College pops up. "They apparently went to the same college as well."

"Where did they live?" I ask.

Logan starts typing again, digging deeper into their history. "Both lived on Brompton Avenue, next door to one another. Give me a second to bring up the exact location."

"Why are you so worried about Had?" I ask, watching screen after screen pop open on the secondary monitor. It borders on headache inducing.

"There we go."

The screen in front of me shows the houses and ownership listing.

"What am I looking at?"

"Schlect's household was in Ruby Schlect's name until her death in 2012. Everything transferred to her only son Karl. He sold the house the following year. Brandy's house is still under the ownership of Maria Brandy. According to this, she's still alive and in her sixties. Husband worked for the government at Northrop Grumman until the late nineties, when he was laid off. According to this, they got divorced, she kept the house, and he moved to Washington DC for a new job. She was a teacher in the school district until she retired."

"Where the hell was all this information before?" I ask.

"We weren't looking for it. We had specific parameters to search. You know we can only provide what you ask for, right? Computers and forensics don't just magically create evidence to suit your needs or jumpstart or finish your case," Logan says.

"I know that. I-I'm more pissed at myself. I just wonder why we didn't think to look for this."

"No reason to. Like I said, the evidence led us one way and we followed it."

I grab the well-worn photo from the pile and hand it to Logan. "Can we do anything with this? Seems to be the best shot of their faces. I thought that would help."

"It's possible, but I can't make any promises."

"I just need the best you got. We need to know who the girl in the photo is."

Logan snaps on his latex gloves before taking the photo to a high-powered scanner. Hitting several buttons, he waits for the image to show up on the wall in front of me. He brings the photo out and places it in a plastic bag, sealing it from the elements. He pulls off the gloves and tosses them in the trash.

"God, I'm tired of fucking gloves." He sits down and begins inputting the image into a facial recognition database. "You think she's our missing woman?"

"I hope so," I reply, my face glued to the screen in front of me. "Check everything—missing persons, DMV, whatever we have access to. Just run it all."

"That might take longer than we have."

Logan crops the image and adds several points to her face, creating a computerized mapping of the contours of her skin. The photo slides to the left of the screen as the computer runs through facial recognition.

"If it's too much, can we narrow it down to the DMV in Nassau County with a Garden City address? Is that possible?" I ask, turning around to stare at Logan's back as he focuses on the screen in front of him.

"That won't be necessary," he says. He clicks a few pictures and the screen behind me beeps. The image of a missing person's report for a Spencer Mere fills the entire screen.

"According to her file, she went missing in 2012. Last seen a week after graduating with her MBA," he says.

"Files online?"

I can hear Logan clicking away as I read the report listed on the screen. There's minimal information. I need that report to determine who was interviewed during the investigation.

"It was scanned last year. I just sent you the link," he finishes as I run out the door, holding a thumbs-up over my head as I go.

***

Frankie sits in my office chair, reading through a file on the desk. Without saying a word, I roll her chair away from my computer and load up my email. After what seems like thirty or so clicks, I pull up Spencer Mere's file and start scanning.

Missing since 2012, last seen leaving a graduation party. Due to the hazy memory of those in attendance, the eyewitness testimony is suspect at best. Several kegs and bottles of hard liquor were found by the bar, as well as a white substance on the coffee tables. Tests confirmed cocaine, but no one could remember who brought it with them. Overall, it was a party that got out of hand with no police involvement until the disappearance was reported.

The last two to see her alive were Schlect and Brandy. Subsequent interviews were brief and, based on the notes, useless. Maria Brandy vouched that both boys were home when Spencer disappeared. Both of their cell phones pinged off a tower right near their house—no ransom calls, no demands. She just fell off the face of the earth.

Handwritten notes on a small piece of paper show the unanswered questions the detectives had. Runaway? Murder? No credit card use. No real paper trail. No trace left behind. Someone had to help her, but who?

"How can a young woman just fall off the grid?" I ask Frankie.

"Year?"

"2012."

"Although it might seem a bit difficult to understand, some people just walk away from technology altogether. It happens."

"That doesn't make sense for a woman like the one who was in all of these photos. She just graduated with her master's degree. Why walk away?"

"Again, any number of reasons. I'd need more information to try and help you. Who are we talking about?"

"Spencer Mere. She went to college with Brandy and Schlect. She's in a ton of photos Brandy kept in a box at the bar. I think they might have done these murders together, but it goes against everything I was trained to know. Psychopaths aren't known to work with a partner in most—if not all—situations."

"Unless he was a pawn. A second in command. Not powerful enough or strong enough mentally to overtake the leader but allowed to stay around for the pleasure of the leader," she says. The pieces begin to click into place in my mind.

"If they've been doing this since they were in their twenties . . ."

"Logically, there could be more bodies you've never known about."

"Locke!" I scream at the top of my lungs. She comes rushing into the office with Zeile and Will on her heels. "We're going to Garden City. Cap, we'll need local cops at this location, and see if we can get a warrant immediately." I hand him a piece of paper with the scribbled address.

"Give me five minutes and I'll come with," Will says.

"You're not cleared yet," I say, and grab my NYPD jacket.

"You're not doing this alone!"

"Did you not just hear me tell the cap we need locals for backup? Locke is cleared for field work." I place my hand on his bicep. "We don't have time for this. Please."

Will knows I'm right and relents. "I'll have Logan track Shawn Brandy's cell phone. See if it's on and pinging."

"Thanks, partner. Let me know if it is. Frankie, let me know if anything jumps out at you in that file. We're kind of going in blind here, but we're running out of time."

Before they can say another word, I'm out the door with Sydney hot on my heels. She grabs an NYPD jacket off a random officer's desk as we head down. I can hear her promising to return it. I know we need to hurry. If Spencer Mere is being held captive in the Brandy home, how did Maria not know about it? We need to err on the side of caution and consider her an accomplice. Either way, I'm not alone. Not this time.

Chapter Thirteen

Out the car window, the rows of houses, varying in size with a good amount of property and trees, zip by one after another. The newer McMansions that cover most of their postage stamp of land stand out compared to the older homes. These original builds from decades ago seem to mimic one another—cookie-cutter homes. The only real difference seems to be the location of the driveway and front door.

Some are more modern than others, but this is your average suburban neighborhood. It's one of the things people love so much about the New York City area and Long Island: the diversity within the monotony. The variations of skin tone on this block alone represent more of America than most people see in a lifetime out West. The freedom of expression in hair color, religious decorations in gardens, the massive trucks in one driveway compared to the small, ultra-compact in another . . . it washes over you that we can truly live together—all of us.

Even with the issues Nassau County has with its government, expensive real estate, and high taxes, I've always wished to bring Chase back home. I want him to grow up where my brother Henry—his father—and I did. He could run in the same parks, walk in the same streets, enjoy the same simplicity of life.

"Steele," Sydney calls as she slows the car. "That's the house." It's a beautiful, two-story, ranch-style house slightly farther down the street. The white horizontal siding is old and bulging on the sides, but clean. The red window shutters have faded from years of sun exposure, but the windows are pristine. The front porch has hanging flower baskets every few feet. It looks like the quintessential all-American house without the white picket fence.

Across the street, two black sedans are idling. I assume the captain told them to be discreet, which would explain the lack of visible cruisers. Still, I wish they would have parked a few houses away. Sydney turns the engine off and the two of us head to the first vehicle. When I tap on the driver's side window, the woman lowers it slightly.

"Get in," she says. Sydney and I quickly slide in the back seat.

"I'm Detective Steele and this is my partner Detective Locke. I assume you're from NCPD?"

"Detective Fleming, and this is my partner Detective Salinas. Detectives Moran and Bradley are in the car behind us. Captain told us to be at your disposal but be inconspicuous. We've got officers around the block waiting for the call should we need them. Want to give us the details of the situation?"

"We have reason to believe a woman is possibly being held against her will at this property. Our investigation into the Carnation Killer led us to his childhood best friend and business partner, who grew up in this house. His mother still lives here, and we don't have a warrant yet," I answer.

"You got this from the guy who was shot in front of your precinct?" Salinas says.

"Yeah, well, before that happened, he told me of his first victim, one he would brutalize on a weekly basis."

"And you're sure he wasn't talking out his ass? I mean . . . criminals lie. It's part of who they are," Salinas continues.

"Until proven otherwise, we prefer to assume she's alive and real," Sydney says.

"Did you run the plates of the car in the driveway?" I ask.

"Yeah, registered to Maria Brandy," Fleming answers. She hands Sydney and me small boxes. "Those are your earpieces and a small battery-operated microphone."

I slip the battery pack in my back pocket and run the wire through my shirt and clip it to my bra. I leave my shirt untucked to hide everything. That, along with my jacket, makes them nearly invisible. Popping the small device in my ear, I instantly hate the feeling of it. Sydney and I hand both boxes back, and Fleming drops them into the center console.

"Everything's set up to the right frequency, so we'll all hear you loud and clear. When you get outside, do a quick mic check. If one fails, just don't go getting separated. They're sensitive enough to piggyback if necessary."

I nod and exit the car. My footsteps barely register on the newly tarred street leading to the postcard-perfect house. "Fleming, can you hear me?"

"Loud and clear." Her voice rings loudly in my ear.

"Locke checking in," I hear in awkward stereo as Sydney checks in.

"All clear," Fleming says.

Heading up the stairs into an unknown environment has usually been my forte, but right now I am not happy to be doing this. As I push the doorbell, the lights above me flash, as do the ones that I can see through the door glass.

An elderly woman opens the door with a large smile on her face. It's then that I notice the sticker on the windowpane near the door. The woman is deaf. There was no indication of that in the file that I saw. It would put the alibi into question immediately. They had to know this when they interviewed her, and it's another reason to continue with the investigation. My blood boils a bit before I calm down and smile at the woman in front of me.

Having no conversational knowledge of sign language or time to wait for an interpreter, I have to use what's available. Pulling out my cell phone, I type a quick message asking if she's Maria Brandy. I hold it up for her to read. She nods with a slight questioning look in her eyes.

I pull out my badge and show her my photo before pointing to myself. Sydney holds hers out as well. The woman leans forward and squints as she takes in the information in front of her. When she leans back into the doorway, her arms cross in a defensive manner. This might be more difficult than I thought.

I write on my phone quickly, asking if she would be willing to help us with the cold case of Spencer Mere. She loosens her arms a little bit and motions for the two of us to come in. After closing the door, she walks over to the couch and points for us to sit down. Once we're seated, she motions to her mouth as if holding a glass. I shake my head no but say thank you in sign language, the only words I really know.

She sits across from us, and I type on my phone and ask her if she knew Spencer Mere. I hand her my device, and she leans back as if carefully pondering her answer. She types her answer and hands it to me.

Her answer is simple: *yes.*

Knowing I have to save all this information for future reference, I continue on the next line. I ask if Shawn was friends with Karl and Spencer. I hand her the phone, and once again she takes a few seconds before handing it back to me.

Another simple *yes.*

I ask about their relationship. Were they all friends or more?

Her answer: *They met in college and became friends. Karl dated Spencer the entire time.*

More information I didn't have before. If she broke up with him, it might stand to reason he would want to keep her around as long as possible to get revenge.

Did Shawn like Spencer? I type out on my phone.

Maria tilts her head, thinking. She types out a few lines, but then stops, rethinks, and deletes everything. She types again for a few seconds before handing the device back to me.

Her answer is longer this time, more involved. *Spencer would have been better off with Shawn, but he would never do anything to break his friendship with either of them. They were three peas in a pod.*

Did he love her? I follow up.

She nods ever so slightly.

Fleming's authoritative voice rings in my ear. "Everything alright, Steele? You're awfully quiet in there." Sydney looks at me, signifying she's heard this too. Sydney nonchalantly turns as if to gaze around the room and whispers, "She's deaf. We're typing on Steele's phone."

"Roger that. Let us know if you need anything," Fleming replies, a bit calmer.

Continuing with Mrs. Brandy, I ask about the last night Spencer was seen alive. Her eyes close, and it seems like she's reaching into the depth of her memory to give me factual information. Either that or a way to bullshit her way out of a poor answer.

My phone rests in my hand as I scan over her answer. *The boys went to meet Spencer at a party for her graduation that night, not too far from here. Shawn came in the front door around one or two in the morning, I think. He told me he would be in his room playing video games. I asked if Spencer was with them, and he said she was with her friends.*

I ask if the car outside is hers.

She shakes her head and laughs while pointing to herself and fake driving.

I angle my head down as I slowly type on the phone.

"Her son set up a car in her name?" Sydney asks.

"Wouldn't be the first time a criminal did that to cover his tracks," I mumble so my lips barely move.

"I'll call it in," Fleming says in my ear.

I hand Maria my phone, asking if her son still comes to visit her. She nods as she types out her answer. *Yes, once a week.*

I ask if Karl does as well. She nods and points to her previous answer before shaking her hand a bit. I don't quite follow, so I type in a question mark. She grabs my phone. *Every other week, but not this time. Shawn came back instead. My boys take good care of me.*

I ask if Shawn is on the property.

Her answer goes back to a simple one: *Yes.*

I ask where.

His man cave in the basement.

I type one more line asking if we can speak to him. She nods and types out her answer. I thank her again before getting up to leave. Sydney follows, me unaware of anything. I'll have approximately two minutes to fill everyone in before heading into the basement.

On the porch, I wave to Maria and put my hands together in a gesture of thanks and bow slightly before closing the door. I walk a few steps away to ensure she won't be able to read my lips as I talk.

"Okay, everyone, the basement only has a back entrance. Shawn is down there. She said he brought supplies for her and stores them downstairs. Old-school storm shelter entrance. We're going to be sitting ducks, so don't be too far away." My mind is already putting together all the things that could go wrong.

Sydney reads through the conversation with Mrs. Brandy on my phone as I look over at the closed door leading to the hidden basement area. If he's right behind the door armed, we're dead. If he's hiding at the base of the stairs armed, we're dead. Our only hope is that he's further inside and unarmed.

"We each grab a side, pull it open, and stay down. Then we'll check, got it?" I say to Sydney. She nods. "Okay. On three," I say.

Both of us grab a handle before I mouth *one, two, three*. Both sides spring open, but nothing happens. Using my phone's mirror app, I look down the steps. Seeing nothing there, I motion to Sydney. The two of us slowly descend the stairs, guns raised and checking in every direction.

At the base of the steps, I realize how big the place is. The massive space has storage shelves on the left that lead to a door. Stacks of water, toilet paper, paper towels, and other cleaning supplies cover the entire shelving system. I motion Sydney to the door in front of us. She nods, walks in front of me, and stands next to the door, hand on the knob—waiting. Once in position, I nod, and she whips open the door. I dart inside the bathroom, gun raised at a mirror, and almost fire at my reflection.

Catching my breath, we walk into the rest of the empty space. A couch and a television with various game systems below it rests along one wall. There's a kitchen nook with the bare essentials: stove, sink, and a small fridge. Two more doors are on the other side of the room. We slowly creep toward them.

One of them has additional padlocks all over it, and the door feels colder than the others to the touch. I point to the other door. Sydney quietly opens it so that we can verify no one is in there waiting for us. Just a desk, file cabinets, and random boxes fill the place.

Stepping back from the doors, I whisper into my microphone. "We're in the basement. There's a door down here with several open padlocks hanging on their clasps. He's got to be in there, so be ready," I whisper.

"On the side of the house, on your mark," Fleming says quickly.

I silently edge up to the side of the door and point to the doorknob again. Sydney grabs it, raises her gun, and mouths the countdown. On three, she pushes the door open, and I rush inside with my gun raised. Immediately, my feet slip out from under me, and my head slams into the floor. I see Sydney stop and remain outside. My vision is a bit hazy, but my hand is coated red with blood.

"No need for a bus. Call the medical examiner," Sydney tells the rest of the team.

"Everybody, stand down. Salinas, handle the call to the coroner. I'll make sure Mrs. Brandy doesn't leave the house." Fleming's voice hurts my throbbing head.

Sitting upright, I come face to face with Spencer Mere, lying on her stomach with her face directly staring at me. Her naked body showcases the bruises of years of abuse. Her eyes are gray and glazed over, her lips solidly blue. My stained hand reaches for a pulse and finds none under the ice-cold skin. The fluid beneath her sliced throat is dry and flakes off when I remove my fingers.

Beyond her rests the body of Shawn Brandy. I move forward and grab a small end table, using it to stand up, my bloody handprint adding to the evidence to be collected in the room. I lean forward and press my fingers to his neck. No pulse, but his skin is still lukewarm to the touch. Both of his wrists are a mangled mess of meat from the straight razor resting in his right hand.

The scene is rife with the sadness of a tormented woman who was tortured for the last few years. Her face is twisted and resigned, as if she knew the end was near. The positioning of the bodies suggests Brandy killed her in an act of rage during intercourse. He then finished himself off by committing suicide. That would explain the grotesque look of pleasure that seems to be etched on Shawn's face.

Useless and unnecessary. That is all I can think of as I hear more voices coming down the stairs. She didn't have to die. Shawn was facing a ton of other charges, so I understand his cowardly way out. But Spencer—he could have just let her let go. My emotions feel somewhere between a pure, raging scream and a bleak numbness. I hate this resolution. Absolutely hate it.

Looking in the mirror, the amount of blood coating my hair and clothing becomes clear. The blood soaking around my boots is reminiscent of the precinct earlier, Schlect's body lying faceup, blood pooling around him. I feel as out of control now as I did then.

If General Smith had just been patient, we might have caught him. We could have found a way, but one man decided to avenge his daughter's death and indirectly took another father's daughter away. I know it will continue if people let grief take over and they stop thinking about the bigger picture. Maybe it's the way of the world nowadays. They want justice so badly, they'll destroy everyone around them to get it. Consequences be damned.

"Steele?" Sydney says behind me.

"Yeah?" I almost whisper.

"Crime scene unit's here. They have clothes for you to wear. Fleming said you can shower at the Twenty-Fifth before we head back. The coroner is transporting the bodies to Victor per Zeile's request."

"Thanks."

I turn away from the bodies and step into the main living area. Two people in white hazmat suits meet me and slowly remove my clothing. Normally this would be intrusive and humiliating, but I feel on autopilot, my rage fading into sadness. My hair gets combed through, which hurts like a bitch, before being put in what looks like a clear shower cap.

As I climb into the back of one of the two CSI trucks, I see Maria on the porch crying into Fleming's arms, her screams reaching everyone's ears but her own. She had no idea what her son was actively participating in. She's all alone now in a world that can't communicate with her. She's been victimized as much as the women they killed. All attacked and harmed in the name of a grotesque pleasure masquerading as love.

The doors close and we lurch forward. I allow my eyes to close and darkness to fill my view.

Chapter Fourteen

Courtrooms have never been a comfortable location for me. Between the idiotic lawsuits that should never happen to the high-level crimes that I'm forced to testify in, they're not for the faint of heart. After my testimony against General Smith, I've been sitting in a small conference room the district attorney said I could hide in.

The media blocks most of the entrances. Beyond that there are protestors for both sides of the equation. Some of them view the murder as a means to an end: less taxpayer money wasted on the hunt and subsequent housing of Schlect. Others feel Smith deserves punishment, but leniency. I see the law as a simple case of black-and-white. The US Constitution doesn't mention it by name, but murder is still against the law in every state. Even though he pleaded not guilty, I don't see how any of the logical defenses could apply in his case. His was an emotional response, but one he planned and understood. The fact that he remained at the scene after the shooting gave credence to this.

The lawyer's words made me want a drink so bad it hurt. He kept drilling the what-ifs into my head. If Schlect had lived, would we have found Spencer Mere alive? If Schlect lived, could we have arrested him for the murders? The list went on, but the pressure of the unknown was palpable. I answered as truthfully as possible.

The reality of the situation is I really don't know. Sure, in theory, it makes perfect sense. I could have followed him, and maybe he would have tripped up somewhere down the line and we could have found her. Conversely, he might have killed several other women before we even got close enough to get a warrant.

It's a no-win argument that people will discuss for years to come. The only thing I know for sure is that the decision was not Smith's to make. It was the law's. No one is above that. Those little words on a page dictate how we interact with one another. They're not difficult to follow, but we are not the judge, jury, and executioner. Not Smith. Not me. Not Schlect. We have a method, a drawn-out, overly filled-with-red-tape process that is meant to ensure innocence before guilt. That is meant to ensure justice. Justice or not, this case will echo in my conscious for some time.

The conference room door opens and there's Frankie. "Penny for your thoughts?" she asks.

"Do you think I might have caught him if I had more time?" I ask.

"I don't know." She sits next to me. "Why do you ask?"

"Would someone else have gotten hurt because it took so long to find them? Because I never spoke up?"

"Jasmine, I don't understand where this is coming from."

I slide around in my chair to face her, my eyes focused on my hands in my lap. "When I was a kid, my best friend Di and I would hang out at her house all the time. We would pretend we were superheroes or famous actors or singers. We'd stay in her basement, where her father built this whole kids' playroom. We'd play there for hours, laughing and just being kids, you know?"

Frankie reaches forward and takes my hands in hers. I look up at her, and I can feel the pressure of tears behind my eyes. My face feels warm, my chest heavy, and I'm starting to sweat.

"I was twelve when we were hanging out. I think we were watching a movie or something on TV, I don't quite remember. Her father came down and told Di to go upstairs and help her mother get dinner ready. I offered to help, but he told me to stay there and relax." The tears start to fall, and I try to look anywhere but at my fiancée. For her part, she does nothing but stay silent and supportive.

"I don't remember much, but his . . . it was never inside. Just hands, touches, kisses . . . things like that, you know? Every time I tried to find the courage to tell anyone, I'd just clam up. I mean who would believe a kid who wanted to tell stories for a living? When I finally spoke up to someone I trusted, they didn't take me seriously. So I locked it away. I pretended it never happened, and each time I went to their house, it did. Happen again, that is. Then I'd go home, take a hot bath and a ton of pain meds, say it was someone else, not me, that it had happened to, and move on."

"Baby . . ." she starts.

"Please, just . . . we went to *that bar* in college. It reminded me of everything . . . because he was sitting there. He was there and hitting on another young girl. I kept thinking if I had put him away, this person wouldn't be a possible victim. That if she was, or had been . . . hurt, then that was on me," I stumble through my tears, my voice shaking as I gasp for air. "You know, he didn't even recognize me. He saw me and offered to buy me a beer. I could feel his breath on my neck. It made me feel so small again, like I was in that basement with the musty smell and his hands down my pants. I left the bar without saying a word. I'm sure he went back to that girl and took her home. I let her become a notch on his belt."

"And when you went to Dreamers Den and saw the same thing, it hit you hard."

"Yeah, and then the lawyer today asking me that? God, I'm no better than General Smith. I wanted Di's father dead. I still want to resurrect him just to shoot his dick off."

"It's not your fault," she says. "None of this was ever your fault. He had control over his own actions. You were only a child."

"I know that, but I promised no more secrets, and you've been patient. After my friend didn't believe me, I never told anyone. Not my mother, grandmother . . . hell, not even my doc later in life. I need you to know this anxiety I get is never going to stop if I don't face it. I managed to hide it for so long, but I don't want to anymore. I need to deal with it. The nightmares, memories, all of it. I need you to be there. You're the only thing that grounds me, and I don't think I can do this—not without you. You need to know I'm still a broken mess. You love me anyway, right?" I finish and drop my head on her shoulder, letting the full weight of my confession fall away.

"I love you no matter what." She pauses, kissing my head. "I'm here, and I'm not going anywhere. Whatever happens, I'll be here to hold your hand, wipe your tears. For forever and a day." Frankie pushes me back gently and places both her hands on either side of my head. "I know we've talked about a big wedding . . . Well, my dream wedding with a live band, cocktail hour, the long white train, and tons of guests."

"I don't think I know enough people to fill up my side of the aisle." I try to laugh, but it sounds more like a forced snort as I can barely breathe.

"I don't need that, any of it. All I need is you—flawed, broken, stubborn, old you. And our son."

"Nephew."

"We didn't give birth to him, but we're raising him, and we love him as if he's our own. I consider him my son, and if he calls me his mama again, I won't correct him, and neither will you. It's his choice. Understood?"

"Yes, ma'am."

Frankie lets go of my face, reaches into her bag, and grabs a tissue. I wipe my face before blowing my nose. After a few tissues get used and tossed in the trash bin, she stands and fixes her black pencil skirt.

"Come with me." She extends her hand.

"Where are we going?" I ask.

"Please just trust me?"

Without saying another word, I take her hand and we walk out of the room. The hallway is still crowded, probably from another case letting out. Frankie takes a hard right, opens a door, and we head up the stairs.

"I love you more than life itself. You know that, right?" She stops on the third-floor landing. "Right?" she asks again.

I nod in reply, not trusting the words that might come out of my mouth.

"Good. I set this all up before . . . well, the conversation we had downstairs. So, if you say no, it's okay. I promise." She opens the entryway and heads three doors down. She walks into another room where a secretary is almost blinding me with her overly whitened, toothy smile.

"What is this?" I ask, my throat still sore from crying.

"I don't want the fanfare. I just want you, our friends, and my family. That's it." She motions behind her, and I can see her father in a suit with Waylon behind him. I notice Wade missing and silently question Frankie.

"He asked for more time. I'll give it to him, but I won't stop living my life while he comes around. Not anymore."

Will steps forward in his Marine blues, his hands resting on the shoulders of Chase, who's wearing dress slacks and a button-down shirt. His father's blue-checked tie hangs slightly askew, and it looks absolutely perfect.

"Frankie . . ." I start, but my heart pounds against my sternum with every breath. "We don't have a license."

"Yes, we do. Plus, the waiting period will be waived by the Honorable Justice Powell if you agree to marry me right here and now," she finishes.

Without saying another word, I take her hand in mine and walk into the judge's chambers. It's then I see Hadley, Logan, Victor, Lillian, and Captain Zeile standing on what would be my side of the aisle. My chosen family, standing there to represent me.

"Mia and the girls send their love. They couldn't make it back from her mother's in time," Will says softly next to me.

I say nothing but continue to take in the people around me. Justice Powell stands in front of his desk, book in hand, waiting for us.

"Hadley, would you be my maid of honor?" I ask, finally opening my mouth to speak to those around me.

She smiles and wraps her arms around me in a gentle hug before standing next to me.

"Victor, be my man of honor?" Frankie says and laughs as he proceeds to fix his tie before kissing her cheek and taking his place next to her.

"Finally," Justice Powell begins. "I've known you both by reputation and have had the pleasure of speaking with you over the course of your careers. It's an honor to be able to do this for you. So, without further ado, do you have a ring?" he asks, and the realization causes my body to go rigid. Hadley taps my arm and hands me a thin, black, tungsten carbide ring with a slice of diamonds in the middle.

"Apparently, I do," I say as nerves rattle my voice. The group softly laughs around me.

"Place the ring on the end of her finger and repeat after me. I, Jasmine Steele, take thee, Francesca Ryan, to be my lawfully wedded wife. To have and to hold, in sickness and in health, for richer or for poorer, for as long as we both shall live. With this ring, I thee wed."

"I, Jasmine Steele, take thee, Francesca Ryan, to be my lawfully wedded wife. To have and to hold, in sickness and in health, for richer or for poorer, for as long as we both shall live. With this ring, I thee wed." I slide the ring down her finger.

"Dr. Ryan, would you please place your ring on the end of Detective Steele's finger and repeat after me? I, Francesca Ryan, take thee, Jasmine Steele, to be my lawfully wedded wife. To have and to hold, in sickness and in health, for richer or for poorer, for as long as we both shall live. With this ring, I thee wed."

"I, Francesca Ryan, take thee, Jasmine Steele, to be my lawfully wedded wife. To have and to hold, in sickness and in health, for richer or for poorer for as long as we both shall live. With this ring, I thee wed." She slides the thicker matching band on my finger, and I feel everything at once: soaring joy, love, and pride.

"You two have proven that you can have patience with one another. You have shown courage in the face of the unknown together. You have made the commitment to be true to your journey as one unit. It is a blessing, and sometimes it will be hard, but I have faith you two will make it work. Jasmine and Francesca, as you two have promised to love and cherish one another by the vows you have said to each other, it is an honor to declare you wife and wife. You may kiss the bride."

Frankie launches herself toward me with a kiss so powerful it makes my stomach do a somersault. I hear Chase make some discontented sound, and I'm sure Will is covering his eyes. She moves away from me and is instantly picked up by Waylon in a tight hug. Frankie's father walks up to me and holds out his hand. I accept it, and we say nothing. It's a small gesture, and I know it is all for Frankie's benefit, but I'll take it.

Hadley hugs me from behind, followed by Will, and then Chase around my legs. So many hugs and well wishes it almost makes me forget my parents aren't alive to witness this. I wonder if my mother is smiling down on me. It's moments like these that her absence hurts the most. I hope my family is proud of how far I've come, despite how long it took to get here, and how happy I finally am.

"Steele?" Zeile says to me. "Walk with me for a second?"

I walk into the secretary's area, watching my family open up a cheap bottle of ginger ale to celebrate. Their laughter echoes into the hallway.

"The higher ups decided to open up a new task force in conjunction with the FBI. We're going to work with them on varying cases from both departments. It's not a step up or down, so don't worry about your title. Same pay, probably longer hours, and it might include some travel out of state as needed. I can promise you it will include the same lack of gratitude regardless of the outcome."

"Sounds like the normal shifting of chairs and titles when they need to cover their asses. No matter what your preferred sports team might be, it was a pleasure working with you. I appreciate you having my back on these last few cases." The words ring true as I hold my hand out to my boss.

"I'm heading it," he says.

"What? They've shifted you out? Because of Schlect? Can they do this?"

"Yes and no." He raises his hands in a calming manner. "They were rather upset by how everything went down. So, I'm being moved to the subbasement in the new division along with you, Everts, and Locke. We'll have access to all of our regular people for forensics, tech, or psych. The cases come from on high, so they are who we report to directly."

"In other words, the cases no one wants with a tighter leash."

"Maybe, or the ones only we can handle. We're a good team, Steele. Maybe this is an indirect promotion. I think it gives us more leeway to deal with cases our way—with less red tape but still by the letter of the law. I know we're going to get higher profile ones since you are the media's darling detective. No matter what, we don't have a choice. Everyone starts on Monday morning. Our stuff is being moved as we speak," he finishes.

"Windows?"

"Nope."

"I don't like it."

"Neither do I."

"Do I still have to call you Captain or is Thomas on the table?"

He laughs and pats me on the shoulder. "Call me Thomas and I'll use your head to make a window. I'm still the captain of our unit; never forget that." He squeezes my shoulder as he smiles brightly. "Congrats on marrying Dr. Ryan. She's a good one, so don't fuck it up." He lets go of me and slides his hands in his pockets as he leaves the room.

Will comes outside and hands me a small glass of ginger ale. "He told you?"

"Monday morning, yup. How do you feel about it?"

"Might be more interesting. Not just dealing with death anymore," he says and takes a sip of his drink.

"No, but we could get worse cases."

"Like what?"

"The ones with living victims," I answer before walking back into the judge's chambers.

***

Frankie is sound asleep next to me, and I can't help but watch her chest rise and fall. Her face is so calm and beautiful, so free of stress. Her eyes dart back and forth in a deep sleep. It's a blessing I never thought I would ever truly get to enjoy. I know that we planned for this, but having it actually happen is beyond my greatest hopes. My wife is asleep. My wife. Those two words will never cease to cause my heart to swell or a smile to form on my face.

My phone vibrates on the end table next to me with a text message.

It's from Hadley. *I'm downstairs.*

I slide out of bed and throw on a sweatshirt to combat the chill of the cold seeping into my bones.

Hadley stands on my stoop holding a box in her hands, a bag over her shoulder. Her mascara is dried in dark streaks down her face, her hair uncharacteristically wild and out of place.

"I didn't know where to go." She sniffles.

"Did you call Logan?"

"I don't . . . I didn't want . . ."

I grab the box out of her hands and place it on the floor as she comes inside. Her body hits the couch and her arms fold protectively around her.

"What's going on?" I ask, closing the door and sitting next to her.

"I came home and my apartment was a mess." She fumbles for her cell phone, her hands shaking violently. "They got in and left me this." She hands me her phone.

I see you.

The words are written in red, streaky letters on her wall in the living area.

"There are more."

I slide across the screen, bringing up the next image: her bedroom, an utter mess. The bedsheets are missing, what looks like a used condom lying on her pillow. There's clothing all over the floor, ripped or—more accurately—shredded.

The bathroom is destroyed, with toiletries strewn over the floor. The living room and kitchen look about the same. The window near the fire escape draws my attention. The glass is broken, and the bars seem to have been torn off somehow.

"They were cut," Hadley says as I zoom in on the photo. "I haven't been home a lot, so who knows how long they've been working on it. I mean, I've been getting letters for at least six months, so maybe that long?"

"Letters?" I ask and hand the phone back to her. She simply points to the box. "That's why Logan was asking if I spoke to you."

"I've been on the road promoting the new film, but he's been worried. He keeps trying to find where they all come from, but the production company said to keep him away from it. They didn't want the bad press," she says. "I don't want him to get hurt."

"That's why you came here." She nods, and I pull her head to my shoulder in a tight hug, allowing my clothing to absorb her tears. "I know my couch isn't that comfy, but it's yours until we get to the bottom of this."

I grab my cell phone from my sweatshirt pocket and send a quick message to Zeile explaining the situation and asking him to have someone search her apartment for clues of any kind. The reply is almost instantaneous.

On it. Fill me in ASAP.

"How's it feel to be married?" Hadley asks, changing the subject as she shakes in my arms.

I grab the blanket off the back of the couch, cover her up, and slide to the end. She drops her head to my lap as I lift my feet to rest them on the coffee table.

"Feels like I can finally breathe," I say and start to run my fingers through her hair. "Now you rest. I'll stay awake and keep you safe."

"You don't have to. I can make coffee." She yawns.

"Sleep."

It takes a few minutes before her soft, stuffy snores fill the living room. Life once again reminds me that it is never done with any of us. We all have happy moments, but to truly appreciate them, we must experience the bad ones. So, I'll stay awake as my wife, best friend, and . . . son sleep safely. It's my job. I accept the responsibility of guarding the door, ensuring only those who treat my family properly are allowed to enter. For the first time in my life, it's one duty I take on willingly and with pride.

THE END

About Author

Kimberly Amato is the author of the Jasmine Steele Mystery Series and Enemy. Having won awards for a TV Pilot she co-wrote & produced, she dove headfirst into writing novels. Always creating, jotting down new ideas & unafraid to try new genres, Kimberly writes mysteries, crime, romance, sci-fi & more. Beyond that, she's a podcaster with her wife, Sheila, for the show Forever Fangirls reviewing TV and film on streaming services and in theaters. Kimberly enjoys keeping in touch with her readers. You can find her by using the links below or going to her website KimberlyAmato.com.

amazon.com/stores/Kimberly-Amato/author/B00RKJDIXA

bookbub.com/authors/kimberly-amato

facebook.com/thekimberlyamato

instagram.com/kimberlyamato

Go to the link below to stay up to date on new releases and more!
https://www.kimberlyamato.com/newsletter

Also By Kimberly Amato

THE STEELE SERIES

Steele Intent (Book 1)

Melting Steele (Book 2)

Breaking Steele (Book 3)

Cold Steele (Book 4)

Steele Shield (Book 5)

Steele Influence (Book 6)

STANDALONES

Enemy